Falling

Other works by Colin Thubron published
by Atlantic Monthly Press

A Cruel Madness
The Hills of Adonis
Journey into Cyprus
Where Nights Are Longest
Behind the Wall

FALLING

Colin Thubron

THE ATLANTIC MONTHLY PRESS
NEW YORK
◆

For Monica

First published in Great Britain in 1989 by William Heinemann Ltd.
First Atlantic Monthly Press edition, February 1991
Printed in the United States of America

Library of Congress Cataloging-in-Publication Data

Thubron, Colin, 1939–
    Falling / Colin Thubron.
    ISBN 0-87113-427-6
    I. Title.
PR6070.H77F35   1991   823'.914—dc20   90-854

The Atlantic Monthly Press
19 Union Square West
New York, NY 10003

FIRST PRINTING

1

This is nothing like I was told. It is not an ordeal, but a thinning away. As the warder accepts my clothes, he barely acknowledges me, only gestures for me to sit down again. Clothes were my last distinction, and now they're gone. He mutters my name once, then lists the folded pile of my unwanted existence: shirt, trousers, wallet, one pair of shoes (black), watch (there will be no Time here), two pens, a diary.

I see him take them away. The medical orderly has finished. 'You can dress now.'

These new clothes are clean, shapeless. The blue- and white-striped shirt is too small; the slip-on shoes (laces a suicide risk) flap about my heels. The vests and grey pullover are inscribed with the Prison Department's initials. They have been worn by so many others that they seem now to belong to nobody. All their colours are pale. I am No. 63176.

My hands tremble as I pull them on. Yet I feel relief spreading through me. Without the crust of dress, I have become almost invisible. I leave myself behind on the warder's documents. I am nobody, really.

The warder hands me to another. 'He's on the thirds. Number twenty-nine.' We climb a stairway into the triple-galleried heart. It is almost silent. Light pours in from the skylit roof and the windows at either end. Our feet ring on the steel. It is like a cathedral.

I realise that I have never dreaded it. This diminished sense of self (of which Clara spoke) is my reward. I needn't make any more decisions. I've made enough already. The echo of my own feet surprises me.

The warder is talking about regulations. 'Slop buckets to be emptied at the following times . . . one shower a week by statutory right . . . a second is permitted . . .' The cell door shuts behind me.

It never closes again as it does that first time. Then you understand why they call this the slammer. The noise haunts you forever. The door itself is a swinging armament of bolts and mortises, with a judas-hole and a reinforced panel in the centre, now sealed, where food used to be pushed through. Its shutting announces that you have become an animal – something which is locked up, let out under observation, locked up again. But this first time, it closes less with a single clang than like the echo of many doors reverberating shut one after another; the noise seems to go on for ever, as if every stage of your life were finding its definitive end.

And you are left on the other side. The room is just five paces long, two paces wide. The air is static: it exists in a composite cube and cannot get out. I stand in it, waiting. The walls are plastered in a salmon-coloured wash, spattered with Sellotape marks from torn-down pin-ups. There is an iron bunk, a wooden locker, a mirror, a chair, a cork notice-board, a slop-bucket. That's all.

Except silence. Silence is what you are shut in with. Beyond the door, or in the cells to either side, men may be screaming and you will not know. Each cell is a bank safe, locked in its own air, its own silence.

My window hangs in a semi-circle at the end. If I climb onto the chair and press my forehead against the bars, a vertical section of the world rises into view. It is like staring through blinkers. I glimpse the roofs of two outbuildings, and a tarmac courtyard under the perimeter wall. The wall is twenty-five feet high, topped with coils of razor-wire and a heavy revetment. Beyond it I can see three council houses and a disused church, then more roofs, and television aerials. The lives lived there are already unimaginable. One of the town streets must run beneath the wall, because the traffic booms there like a distant waterfall.

It will grow harder to look out of this window, I think. At once I feel that spasm in my stomach (whoever said the seat of the emotions was the heart?) and want to be sick. I climb down again. I stoop over the slop-bucket expecting to vomit, but nothing comes. I wonder how many times, over how many months or years, this has to happen before I realise that she is not out there.

These first hours are meant to be the worst. It is the deprivation of freedom which stuns, they say: the animal humiliation of it. But I can't feel that. This blankness of walls, of clothing, of time, is the condition of my survival. Nothing. I learn to walk in patterns up and down the linoleum. I have not the concentration to read (although we are allowed six books.) But as the hours pass, my cell changes. At first it is only the door which matters. The walls converge on it, flow away from it. The door is life. But there are no bolts, no handles even, on this side – only the judas-hole, where a warder's eye shows once, then goes away. So little by little the door's immobility blends it to the rest of the cell, and slowly, instead, the room begins to turn around the window: a smear of cloud. But I am starting to avoid it, the outside, and what it does not contain. I decide not to stand on the chair again, or not yet. By lowering my gaze as I walk I exclude the barred rectangle of sky. And now it is the walls which really compose the place. And the squares of linoleum between my feet. Four . . . six . . . six . . . four . . .

Once I stare at the mirror. Impersonal in the pale-striped shirt, he stares back at me. The wide forehead is helmeted in short, dark hair, and the pugnacious chin is rudely familiar. But between them, the face has collapsed inward. Lines plough from the eyes' corners down to the jaw. The cheeks are gulleys, the eyes dead and glaring. And I am only thirty-three. Frightened, I try to smile at the reflection. It grimaces back. I hang a towel over the mirror.

Nothing now disturbs this peace.

At eleven-thirty the prisoners are unlocked to slop out their buckets and queue for lunch. I see them for the first time. Us. My eyes make no contact with theirs. I register a line of men such as might queue up in any factory canteen. Only quieter. I had expected shame, defiance or hurt. Instead I gauge no mood. I don't think there is one. I keep my gaze on the back of the man in front of me. His neck is tattooed with wings. Only those prisoners who dole out the minced meat and spinach grin and joke a little. We are locked into our cells to eat. Our precautionary plastic knives and forks are combined absurdly with sharp-edged metal trays. At four-thirty we are released again to take high tea to our cells and slop out our buckets in relays. By six-thirty everybody is locked up again for the night. And still I have not spoken with a soul. I keep my light on until midnight, because I don't know what to do with the dark. I wonder how long I will continue like this. I cannot write what I dream.

At seven-thirty in the morning it starts again: slop out, breakfast, lock-up, slop out, lunch . . . At eleven-fifteen a warder inspects my cell on a routine check of bars and locks. At one-twenty another shouts in: 'You've got a visitor,' as if I didn't know.

I have been preparing for an hour, although there's really nothing to do. I'm probably cleaner and more closely shaven than I often was outside. Now I comb and pat my hair into gentling shapes. But in the mirror I look decapitated by the prison pullover, my head stranded above it like some memory-trace. I rub my cheeks in my palms, to soften out the lines, and turn away before they reassemble. I am struck by the idiocy of this. It's like polishing a car whose engine has broken.

The visitors' room resembles a cheap cafe. Two officers watch preoccupied from a desk, and a woman serves tea in

4

a cubicle. We sit at formica tables with numbers chalked on their edges, facing empty chairs, while the visitors' heads move in outline against the frosted glass of the passage beyond. I cannot yet see hers. For a minute these profiles bow and straighten while their bags are searched. Then they start to trickle through the door: wives, girlfriends, mothers. I cannot imagine Katherine among them. They lug carrier bags of food. Already the couple beside me are bathed in whispers and cigarette smoke, their hands locked. His fingers tap against the sleeves of her blouse. I try to picture Katherine in the doorway, as if this will materialise her, but she does not fit there. On my other side a husband and wife are arguing. He is pale and virulent, trying to dominate even now. She must do this, she will do that. She looks back at him, tired, stubborn. Beyond them a prisoner talks absent-mindedly to his mother, and bounces his two-year-old on his thighs.

Then Katherine appears. For a second she does not look as I remember her at all, and I realise that this moment is torment for her. Her gaze panics round the room before finding me. Then she comes forward and we don't know how to kiss but take each other's hands across the table, and she sits down tentatively, as if the chair might break, and composes her expression.

She comes from a world I no longer know, any more than she can know mine. Our voices sound smaller than they used. We float the words at one another, waiting for them to work.

'How are you?' Her gaze is searching my face. God knows what it finds.

'I'm all right.' I am dead, that's all. Don't try to bring me back.

She covers my hands with hers, as if to warm them. Her face is touched with alarm. She is wondering how much is left of what she remembers. But I can't answer.

*　*　*

We met two years ago, at a party given by the *Hampshire Times*. Its theatre critic was a friend of hers. Among the genial hacks and bleary editors were a few younger journalists, assiduous girls and leather-jacketed men trying to look like investigative reporters. One of these – the one with the open collar and trainers – is me. I recall him with envy. While most of the others slouch or prop themselves against the walls, this buoyant-looking one stands with feet apart, his drink untouched, and is probably cross-questioning somebody. The jaw and deep-set eyes go needling impertinently. He shreds topics as if they were onions (so is often left with nothing.)

People find him too earnest, too aggressive. But in retrospect there is something touchingly boyish in his conviction that nothing is quite what it seems, that everything – events, other people, even himself – must be deeper and more valuable than it is. And there may have been moments when his restless fascination with the world struck people less as a strength than a distress signal.

Yet when I think about him now, it is his sense of purpose which astonishes me – the ravening curiosity which sent him burrowing through countless unrelated subjects in a blizzard of articles, interviews, enquiries, insights and blunders. What drove him? What was the point?

Katherine later confessed that she'd thought me arrogant. She did not realise that my exactingness was the product of retarded education. My father was a land surveyor who died when I was sixteen, leaving my brother and me to care for a bewildered mother. 'She's not a very strong person,' my father used to say (in her defence), but neither were we. I had dreamed my way through school, and now awoke in the adult world with a sudden rage to decipher it. I have no idea why this was. I never questioned that my hunger to understand would last a lifetime. But now that it has gone, it seems mysterious and irrevocable.

Katherine said that I pinned her in a corner and cross-examined her about stained glass (she already had her own studio). I don't remember this. But I do remember thinking how restful she was to talk with, very quiet and serious. I never heard her laugh, but she smiled often. Her features were perfectly regular, lit by chestnut eyes under heavily marked brows. Everything about her seemed calm, almost grave. Even her body. I had the impression that her face – its pale, soft skin texture – belonged in some old-fashioned portrait-frame.

It still does. Her fingers on the prison table have that painterly smoothness. I hold them up teasingly in mine, as I used to do, and deflect the conversation from the mine-field of the past to the neutral present. How is her work?

Stained glass: her passion. Once I wanted to write an article about her, but she never let me. It was too close to her. Sometimes she spoke of these brilliant jigsaws as of a spinsterish hallucination, an infidelity to the real world. Her studio reminded me of a chapel. Apart from two kilns, firing and annealing chambers, it was commandeered by mysterious charts and utensils. It was months before I touched them. Across her work-table spread ox-hair tracing brushes, stipplers, quills, oyster knives, grozing pliers and glass-cutters with tiny carbide wheels. There was a smell like some clinical incense: gum arabic or hydro-fluoric acid.

I found it incongruous that she should be working in the hardness and precision of glass. But the first time I visited her she was so absorbed that she had forgotten I was coming. There was nothing to write about her, she said. But assembled on an easel behind her – huge and iridescent against the light – hung her latest commission. I could not take my eyes from it. 'Are you repairing that?'

'No. It's just . . . unfinished.'

It looked like a chancel window which somebody had broken: a mass of colours burning round a crater. She steered me away from it. I imagined someone intruding on one of my half-finished articles, and thought I understood. She explained cutline drawings to me, and the technique of leading. Then she talked about the different qualities of glass, pulling samples from her shelves like books. I was inducted into the qualities of Streaky and Mixed Opalescent, Reamy and Wispy and Flashed Antique.

'These mouth-blown glasses are quite different from the machine-made ones.' But it was only when she held up two fragments to the sunlight that I realised what she meant. The machine-made was transparent: dead. But the hand-made held the light in the density of its glass. It was a pane of sun. 'The light catches the bubbles, you see, the imperfections.'

Then, half reluctantly, she approached the giant collage in the window. We stood in front of it, like bride and groom. It had been commissioned for a window in the transept of a country church, and she had assembled it by sticking its fragments on the glass with plasticine, and painting in the lead-lines behind. It was arresting and strange. At its foot, on clear glass, was inscribed: 'I beheld Satan as lightning fall from heaven,' and the whole composition was dominated by the downward thrust of sunrays, down through abstract orchards and lounging beasts to – suddenly – a gaping hole, as if some lout had hurled a brick through it.

'I can't make up my mind about that part.'

I moved closer to inspect. It was a vision of judgement and paradise. High in the point of the arch, the presence of God unfolded as an ammonite, whose lozenges and triangles spiralled downwards into the tiers of heaven. Beneath Him, in the laps of the patriarchs, the souls of the blessed lay as swaddled infants, and beneath them again, in the elysium of Isaiah, wolf and lamb, lion and ox, were melded together like different aspects of the same beast.

But it was the tints that were extraordinary. The whole composition was suffused in an autumnal bonfire of colour – sepias and rubies, umber and crimson, marmalade,

8

copper. Even the composite lions and lambs might have been mating or asleep together. The flashed glass of their coats and manes had been delicately sandblasted away to the amber beneath, so that the two animals, yellow and white, blended in a single pool.

This gorgeous pipe-dream touched me with paradoxical melancholy. It struck some spring of nostalgia, I suppose, so that I found myself remembering the parish church of my childhood, which I had last entered at my father's funeral. The glass there was all Victorian (I think) but it emanated the same comfort, the same sense of ineluctable order.

Katherine was frowning. She kept masking off different areas with her palm.

'What's wrong?' I asked. 'I think it's beautiful.'

'Do you? do you, really?' Her gaze came pouring over me (as it does now, in this prison, questioning) but relaxed as she believed me. 'I'm glad. You're almost the first person to have seen it.'

Her smile increased her oddly static beauty. Often this smile remained long after its cause had gone, as if she had forgotten it.

I asked: 'Don't you have anyone to tell you what they think?'

She said non-committally: 'Not often.'

'And what about that?' I pointed to the hole in the centre, from which the glass had been removed, or never set. All her paradise was gathered round this void, but I could now see that it described a falling angel. Two splintered wings and a bent leg were sketched in the false leading, while in the glass above them the Archangel Michael closed his hands on the last blade of light.

'That? That's the problem,' she said. 'I know the shape but not the colour, not even the glass type. It's Lucifer. He has to be absolutely different from everything else.' She seemed slightly angry with him. 'You see, he's falling

9

through Eden. So he must contrast. In the original sketch I painted him pale green, like a snake.'

'What was wrong with that?'

'Those colours always recede. Dark colours come forward, pale ones recede.'

'I suppose he could be red.'

'There's too much red everywhere else.' She bent down to examine the cutline. Her hair parted on a soft triangle of neck. 'I wanted the warm colours for paradise.'

'You didn't begin with Lucifer?'

'Yes.' her voice brightened in self-mockery. 'But I couldn't solve him, so I left him alone. I was too impatient to start on the rest.'

How extraordinary, I thought. Anybody else would have relegated Eden to a foil for the fall of evil. The drama would all have lain in the archangel's victory or in Lucifer's defiance. But not for her. She had postponed Satan, and had plunged instead into the blinding riddle of God: into her elysian orchards and swaddled souls. Perhaps she simply did not find evil interesting. I tried to imagine her days here. While other people spent their week making business deals, supervising conveyor belts, litigating or going on strike, she was accumulating, piece by prismatic piece, this unearthly ideal.

I don't know why I took her hand. It was resting on the easel's edge, and I simply took it. It stiffened, startled, in mine. Then she turned uncertainly. 'Are you laughing at me?'

'Laughing? No. Why?'

'I just thought . . . you seemed . . .' She stared at me, hesitant. I think she was asking: are you messing me about?

This memory starts a pang of guilt. I look at her across the prison table and know that the lines around her eyes were spread there by me. She has brought me gifts – biscuits, shampoo, chocolate. One of the officers is signalling that our time is up. She pushes them towards me. 'I

10

hope you're allowed these.' She smiles. I am unsure whether what she emanates is still her love-need, or simply compassion. Friends sometimes spoke of her as 'good', as others might be described as 'evil'. These concepts have never explained people to me. They simply seem the shorthand of ignorance. But Katherine often used them, and when she did they were curiously reassuring, as if they described something real after all.

We became lovers, and love took on a settled meaning for me. It was not the one I imagined. I had dreamed of a blinding wholeness. Previous affairs had dwindled away in the absence of that. But with Katherine this absence was masked by the presence of something else: something hard to identify. It was like recognition. With her I felt that I was returning, reentering some place where I had been whole – or where my family had been whole. We shared the same background, I suppose, and had inherited the same values. That helped, but did not explain it. Sometimes I felt that I had been brought up with her, as if she were the sister whom my brother and I had invented in the nursery, to play tricks on. Often I would find her reading authors or listening to music I had valued years before, when I had more time.

Our bodies seemed to dovetail in remembrance. Without her habitual loose dresses (I complained of their shapeless-ness) she was heavily beautiful. Beneath me she seemed physically to soften, as if in chemical change. She never achieved orgasm, and said she did not care. Loving to her was a kind of homecoming. She would close her eyes and work her hips around me in a slow dream of her own, murmuring and even laughing faintly (the only times I heard her laugh). But at other times, while kissing my mouth or neck, she would suddenly look in my eyes, checking if I still loved her, and I would sense some fragility rocking her, some half-buried conviction that she was not, in the end, lovable. Sometimes, too, she would abruptly get up and go into the bathroom, and I would hear her washing herself all over, stomach, arms, crotch.

My friends found her conventional and shy. Hers thought me too nervy and exacting. And our weekdays were spent in separate worlds, I returning late to my flat from too-long assignments. But at weekends I would join her in her studio to find that while I had been turning out my fever of articles – published and forgotten in the same week – she had built up a texture here, a colour there, in the recovery of her private paradise.

In the end, our closeness was intangible to me. For all I know, it was more a matter of sharing cheap wine late at night, or burnt toast for breakfast, enjoying sex on waking up, or a passion for Schubert.

It was as if I had spent the past fourteen years questioning, challenging, renouncing, and that somewhere along the way I had lost my original language, which Katherine still spoke. With her those frenetic years seemed no more than the far arc of a circle which was turning back to find itself.

A romantic fallacy, of course.

She stands up and takes my hand. The officer beckons the next visitors. When I submit her gifts for inspection, the shampoo causes trouble. This type can be inhaled as a drug, apparently, and the plastic bottles used for syringes. So they are returned to her. Something about this wrenches me unbearably. She leaves without looking back.

2

I am a model prisoner. Passing time has become my forte. Sleep returns Clara to me, but the moment I wake up I concentrate on some chore. So it is while making up my bunk or scratching at my stubble with a blunt razor (they give out only one a week here) that I remember. I do everything slowly. The emptying of my slop-bucket in the latrines has become a dead-march, and I eat my breakfast with attention to leftover husks of porridge or flecks of scrambled egg. I have no appetite, but you'd think me a famine victim. Then I volunteer for exercise, which is not exercise at all but a sluggish ramble round the yard. Its walls are whitewashed to shoulder height, then go on climbing in grey stone. You can see our block best from here. It rises in a sheer cliff: a quadruple tier of squat windows. Their bars are painted white, but don't quite mesh at the top, and they are underscored by string courses which run almost the length of the façade before tilting up at the corners. This gives the building a grotesque appearance of smiling. Above them the roof falls in a forest of chimneys and razor-wire, and its gutters enter drain-pipes which are sunk deep into the stone's fabric, so nobody can descend them.

I walk a figure-of-eight along the concrete path between the shrubs. I can prolong this for over half an hour. The warders watch us, arms crossed against the cold, ears to their walkie-talkies. Then the 43s are moved in – child abusers and rapists endangered by other inmates – and I am ordered back inside to inaction. But the workshops open at nine-thirty, so for two hours I can stitch mailbags.

I'd imagined this was finished in prisons nowadays, but no. We labour under neon lights, eight stitches to the inch, in near-silence. That way I earn nearly three pounds a day. In our economy, three pounds is worth having.

Everything narrows here. The outer world grows abstract. Its living and dead seem alike. It is a kind of hereafter. So I imagine her outside somewhere.

In my third week an officer appears in my cell. 'You're being moved down to the twos,' he says. 'You'll be doubled up with Morgan. He's no trouble.'

I had expected this. We're so crowded here that nobody remains alone for long. Morgan's cell is the same size as mine but fitted with an extra bunk and locker. The shelf and walls are packed and festooned. It doesn't take much to fill a regulation cell: a few tobacco tins, a centrefold of pin-ups. After my aseptic cell, this one reeks of past inmates: their boredom, spitting, masturbation, despair.

Morgan is an elderly con-man. He sits over an unfinished game of Monopoly, hired from the wing office. His face seems to be falling apart. It goes in three or four different directions. He appraises me, but reserves judgement and says: 'Weren't you in the papers or something?' His lips unfold wetly on a shambles of teeth. 'I mean your case.'

'Yes.' I can imagine him in better days, when his facial muddle was pulled together by a winning smile, and he has a photograph to confirm this. But four years inside have dilapidated him. Behind his spectacles, the iris of one eye drifts to its corner, leaving a bloodshot whiteness, and lends him a look of furtive disarray.

'I've forgotten the details,' he says.

I place my spare clothes in the empty locker and look round the walls.

'If you want to put up your women,' he says, 'you can. Those ones were Steve's.'

'I haven't got any.'

I have a single snapshot of Clara, but it has gone dead.

14

I've looked at it too often. It has simply replaced her. That's what happens.

'Do you want to take Steve's counter?' Morgan is looking at the Monopoly board. 'They ghosted him out so quick he couldn't finish.'

'They what?'

'Ghosted him. Screws took him off in the night. Back to Maximum Security.'

But Morgan has preserved the Monopoly layout, waiting. This fastidiousness is typical, I discover. All his possessions are arranged with such intricate precision that he could live here blindfold. If I disturb anything, he realigns it at once with a petulant 'Aaach!' Every morning, after dangling his feet over the bunk-side and fixing his spectacles, he sits watching for three or four minutes, checking that everything has remained in its place: transistor, tobacco, pot of lanolin, pen, the antacid tablets for his stomach.

He treats Monopoly like a chess tournament. Sometimes we play all evening. It defers the hour of darkness without sleep. Morgan always chooses the top hat as his counter. He likes that image. He shakes the dice interminably in his pallid hands, then releases them as if performing magic. The problem of whether he accumulates houses on Bond Street or exchanges them for a hotel on Piccadilly elicits long, silent calculations. He only buys the more expensive properties. So the game intensifies. It eats obediently at the clock, creating its own time. When one of our counters lands us in jail, we are barely conscious of the irony.

I don't ask him about his past. (I don't want to trade it for my own.) But during the third of these evenings, warmed by his build-up of houses on Mayfair, Morgan lets out: 'This is like the old days.'

'Is it?'

'Yeah. I was in the business, you know. Building. Had my own company.'

'What happened?' I shake the dice over the question.

'Fell into debt. Bad customers, and that. We couldn't wear the receivers looking too hard at us – books weren't too clean, and my partner had done some kyting on the side. So we cleared out.'

I think Morgan has been drinking a bit. There's a private hootch circulating along the twos catwalk – a fermented brew of sugar, flour and raisins – and he has some concealed in a medicine bottle. 'Me and my partner set up trade in another part,' he says. 'We'd rent offices for a month or two and advertise building services. "Major repairs carried out promptly and cheaply: estimates free." That got the custom. I'd give out the reckonings like an old-fashioned brickie – dungarees, pencil-behind-the-ear, you know. Me, I've got an honest face. People always tell me I've got an honest face.' He pauses to buy Regent Street. 'Wouldn't you say I'd got an honest face?'

'You look OK to me,' I say. He looks too pathetic for crime.

'Well, of course we'd need money in advance for building materials. You can't begin without materials, not a small firm like us. Then we'd delay starting – a few weeks, a month – while we got up business. Then one day we wouldn't be there . . .' His good eye swivels at the snapshot on the wall. 'That's us.'

Morgan is standing against a pub bar with his weasel-faced partner and two others. They all have their arms round one another. Morgan looks chipper in a salt-and-pepper suit and the striped tie of some stodgy club or school, and his face has fleshed out around an all's-well smile. 'That's my buddy,' he says, pointing to the weasel. 'He's into the big time now. When I get out he and I'll go into business proper. No bunco, this time. There's opportunities out there in the building trade. Golden opportunities . . . In a year I'll have me a place like he's got – an estate in Bucks somewhere, swimming-pool, limo, the lot . . .'

He winks at the snapshot. Above it, on the cork notice-board, hangs a picture he painted in the evening art class. It is a landscape of gaudy mansions on emerald hills, and he has framed it with cardboard shutters, to create an illusory window in the wall of our cell. It enshrines his daydream. Yet he seems happier inside than anyone else. It's I who get obsessed with space.

Sometimes, because my boundaries are these four walls, I confuse them with grief, and feel that if they were gone I would be all right. Then the claustrophobia rises like a sickness. I dream of deserts and low hills. They have nothing to do with the real world. They're a kind of oblivion. I feel I could extinguish anything by walking over them. But then I'm seized by that longing which seems so maudlin to the unbereaved: to be near the grave. It is a hopeless, animal wish. Because that is the closest you can come, and that is all there is.

I even ask to see the chaplain. If you insert a note in the box outside the wing office, a warder comes and locks you in his visiting-room.

The priest looks like a ginger cat. His face is becalmed in horizontal lines: lines spreading across his forehead, out from a broad mouth, wide-set eyes.

He says: 'I don't think we've met before, have we?' as if I were a parish councillor.

'I only came three weeks ago.'

This jogs his memory. 'Have you settled in all right?' His face softens into professional concern. There is a self-consciousness about him, but I still feel grateful. He is the first person to have looked at me like that.

We talk for a few minutes about fellow prisoners (but I know only a few) and about the regimen. Then he says: 'Perhaps this is a necessary time for you. Like a period of mourning. In most other societies, you know, there's a mourning period.' He puts a hand on my knee. For a second I wonder uncomfortably about this, but the hand is neutral. 'It's possible, you know, to think of a prison

17

sentence as a shriving. Look at it this way, if you like: it's something you give to God.'

'I don't know God.' There's anger in my voice. 'I'm giving it to her.' The words 'Look at it this way' always did infuriate me. In a minute he'll say: 'You'll be better off viewing it like this . . .' and I'll be shouting my head off. But he only goes on, with his feline composure: 'She's accountable to God as well. You must face that.'

Clara and God: they don't seem a likely partnership. I remember Katherine's stained-glass paradise: the swaddled souls of the blessed (or were they bandaged?). I try to imagine they hold some meaning. But neither they, nor the priest, seem to mean anything. I wonder now why I wanted to talk with him, and feel that under the Cheshire Cat calm there may be a man I have offended, so I say: 'I'm sorry, Father [why do I call him Father?], I'm not in the right frame of mind. I'll see you later, maybe.'

'That's quite all right. I'll be here most days.'

I turn round at the door before the warder unlocks it. The priest says: 'Did you need something else?'

I want to ask: *Isn't there anything left?*

But instead I say: 'No.'

When I return to our cell, I find Lorrimer there. He's slipped in during the minute between high tea and lock-up to buy hash from Morgan. Most days I see Lorrimer scanning the visitors' lists outside wing office, calculating who's likely to be receiving dope. He used to obtain a half-ounce packet of heroin every time his girlfriend visited. When they kissed goodbye, she would pass it from her mouth to his right under the screws' noses. But now that the girlfriend's left him, he has to go humouring Morgan. Morgan sells hash in 'quarter-ounce deals', which in fact weigh almost nothing. He doesn't like Lorrimer.

I can understand that. Lorrimer is only twenty-four but already looks hardened. He is in here for life. 'Did over a cop during a push-in job,' he says. 'Nearly killed him.'

18

Under his black brows and black hair he looks coldly restless: intense dark eyes, Borstal spots on either cheek, and tattoos lapping up his neck – the kind of uneven tattoos which prisoners self-inflict (I recognise them now), names of girls entwined in genitalia and swastikas. He's harshly intelligent: one of those who keeps his pride by defeating the system – petty drugs trading, murmurings of escape. He exudes a pent-up violence.

I'm a bit in awe of him. A man's size counts here, and Lorrimer is big. Most of the prisoners ignore me, but he'll come up and talk, while all the time fixing me with his unregenerate stare. Now that I'm back from the chaplain he squeezes Morgan's fix into a pouch inside his vest and says: 'You been seeing Holy Joe?'

'Something to do,' I say.

'You don't know where you are with those fellows.' Lorrimer laughs. 'Now with Morgan I know the score, don't I, old chuck?' He ruffles Morgan's hair (Morgan hates this). 'If he floats me a fix of Acapulco gold, I know the going rate. But what is it with these Bible-bangers? They're just in the game of keeping you guilty, making you feel you ought to be in this fucking place.'

Morgan says: 'You should try jackarsing the chaplain, Lorrimer. He might give you a good report. Get remission.'

I'm faintly surprised. 'Does the chaplain file reports?'

'You bet he does,' Lorrimer says. 'Everybody here files reports – screws, medics, probation snoopers, shrinks – you don't exist except in reports. They invent you for the Home Office. That's why people blarney the chaplain. They're after good marks with the governor.' He grinds out his cigarette, pockets the stub. 'Maybe it's worth it for you fellows. But I'm not waiting that long. I'm for the out.'

He's a fool, of course, in the long term. Those few who escape get caught in the end. Morgan looks at him morosely, old with repetitions. 'Better quit trying. Time'll pass.'

But Lorrimer won't give in. He's like a wolf trotting its

cage. I think he has no choice. I warm to him. My other self, who existed before No. 63176, understands that wolftrotting. Lorrimer has years, perhaps, decades, to endure in prison. Yet I realise I envy him. He is bursting with unrepentant purpose. And escape has a meaning for him. His fists are grinding on the Monopoly table. His blackhaired wrists meld unthinned into his hands. All he says is: 'Waiting's all right for some.' Then he makes for the door, before turning to me and asking: 'What are you in for, squire?'

3

It was one of those soft summer nights which come in consolation for days of drizzle. The tent's silhouette winked with pink and amber bulbs along its guy-ropes, and sent up a muffled cloud of music. But the neon lights spelling 'Appleby's Big Top' had mostly expired, leaving dead hieroglyphs above the canopy. I must be running out of ideas, I thought, deciding to report on a circus. Circuses rarely came to Peterhurst, and when they did, they were small.

This one was minimal – a two-pole tent, forty yards by thirty. Inside, it was filled by a nostalgic smell of crushed grass and dung. The audience numbered barely eighty, mostly children, scattered in a thin arc behind the painted boards. I scribbled on a pad in the semi-darkness: 'How on earth does it pay?'

A three-piece band crashed into life from a balcony draped with crumpled curtains. Then the ringmaster appeared. He looked shrunken in his scarlet tail coat, lashing his microphone wire behind him. His voice came hoarse: 'Ladies and gentlemen, welcome to the great-est show on ear-earth . . .'

They seemed to belong to a separate race: men with slicked-back hair and matinee-idol grins, girls in cowboy boots and spangled tights. They bounded across the ring beside a pair of plumed horses – palomino and strawberry roan. As the stallions cantered the sawdust, reared, turned, cantered again, two cowgirls ran to kneel on their backs. One slid off with a yelp. The other stood shakily upright.

They were gone in a splurge of mud and music, the ringmaster shouting for applause.

The next moment somebody carried in a kennel, and a fat woman in a turban released a mob of tiny, shaven dogs. They turned somersaults and bounced over hurdles like mechanical toys, while she let out a shrill 'Yip-yip-yip,' and placed lumps of sugar between their teeth. My notepad fell limp between my knees, and remained there as one act laboured after another. A strong-man paraded with a drugged-looking python. A pair of jugglers dropped their Indian clubs. When the clowns shambled on in outsize shoes, their crosstalk was drowned out by the band. Behind their melancholy, whitened faces I could discern grown men, whose buffoonery must have made them ashamed. No child shrieked at their slapstick. And at each entry the master-of-ceremonies routinely poked the air with his whip, and announced: 'Here come the Magnificent . . .' or: 'Give a welcome to the World-Famous . . .', and on would troop a pair of garish Red Indians or a moth-eaten Shetland pony.

Their energy seemed to have ebbed now. Their smiles grew perfunctory. If it were not for the flashing lights and furious persuasion of the music, I thought, their turns would be pitifully exposed. They seemed to go forward only by a collective act of self-deception in both audience and performers – percussive drums and cymbals, ritual clapping, spotlights, summoned applause and the spurious continuity of the electronic organ.

I watched the children's faces. They were sucking popcorn and candyfloss. What were they seeing? Was this the dazzling circus of my own childhood? I was sure it wasn't. Yet I dimly remembered the same acts: a cowgirl balanced on a palomino; acrobatic pugs in ruffs; a clown sitting on his broken-down car bonnet while water squirted out of his hat.

But something had changed. I could not remember a circus so empty. I felt sorry for its performers. I had the

22

impression that they were mutely desperate. After each turgid success, these garish-costumed girls – a cross between athletes and bar-maids – would fling up one arm in triumph and beam uncertainly. They looked innocent and humiliated.

The Death of the Circus, I wrote in the interval. Has the combined influence of television and the animal welfare lobby finally killed off the circus? It certainly looks like it. The sequence of amateurish acts which Appleby's Big Top brings to Peterhurst green this week confirms that the bell-tent has stayed still while the world has moved on. Nowadays most children, let alone adults, are too sophisticated for . . .

I felt a pang of guilt. The show must be on its last legs. I recognised the couple serving hot-dogs as the man-and-wife juggling team, anonymous in boilersuits. The woman behind the candyfloss counter was the girl who had fallen off the strawberry roan. The ringmaster was in dirty overalls now, raking over the ring.

The lights dimmed again. The cymbals and the Yamaha organ struck up, and the strong-man, dressed as a Hindu fireater, gorged on a flaming torch. Then came the elephants: two sad, tattered pachyderms whose ears had faded to pink. With imbecile slowness they entwined each other's tails, circling the ring, and lifted their tinselled legs onto stools. When they sat down, their haunches and stomachs swelled out obscenely below tiny teats. It was impossible to know if they were bewildered, frightened or at peace. I was aware only of the inelegant sadness of the thing. Once or twice they tilted back their lopped tusks in a soundless roar.

At Peterhurst green this week a cast-iron case was made for the elimination of animals from showbiz . . .

As the show neared its end, and the remorseless clowns interlarded each act, the ringmaster's voice seemed to turn pleading: 'And here, for your entertainment, those mad moonrakers . . . and once again, the desperate duo . . .', but lifted in a little sigh before announcing: 'Now, ladies and gentlemen, will you give a big hand for the amazing, the high-flying, the one and only Clara – the – Swallow!'

There was desultory clapping. She stepped into the ring's centre in a cape and high heels. Her eyes seemed enormous. Her head was encased absurdly in a crown of blue feathers, from which two tiny wings sprouted above the ears. Beside her a thirty-foot aluminium sway-pole had been erected, topped by an iron cradle. It reached almost to the apex of the tent. As she sloughed her cloak and shoes, she shot a smile over the spectators' heads. Her legs were spangled with fishnet tights, and she wore a low-cut turquoise costume, fringed outrageously with sequins.

The band struck up hysterically as she climbed the pole, and a spotlight followed her up into the darkness. When she reached the top, she hoisted herself confidently onto the cradle. It was swaying with a silent, regular roll close under the canopy. She stood up, extended one leg, and held its ankle in an aerial splits. I scribbled: *A bit outlandish.*

Then she bent over the cradle, slid one elbow through its forearm brace, and slowly unfurled into a handstand. The music stopped. For minutes, it seemed, she hung motionless in that tunnel of light, although it could not have lasted ten seconds. Something about her isolation there, curved in a white question-mark, was at once poignant and precarious.

The next moment she was upright again, and the voice of the ringmaster rasped out of darkness: 'Now, I must ask you to be silent while Clara the Swallow attempts . . .'

The band burst into a contradictory rumpus while she released a nine-foot extension to the pole and locked it in place. Its narrow platform seemed to scrape the canvas. There was no safety net; she wasn't wearing a lunge-belt. The music tensed to a scraping of cymbals. But she pulled herself effortlessly up. The shadow of her spotlit body rose to meet her over the tent ceiling. The pole was swinging like an inverted pendulum through a trajectory of six or seven feet. I thought: that girl wants to kill herself. But she stood up defiantly, and I saw the white glint of her smile and eyes. Her feathered crown resembled some grotesque astral bathing-cap. Around me the spectators' faces were gazing up with sleepy respect, surfeited by clowns, and the children went on licking at candyfloss. I wondered: why the hell's she doing it?

The music sounded a corny drum-roll. The cymbals clashed. As her platform swayed through its meridian, her left leg and torso smoothed into an arabesque, and her arms stretched forward. And there she remained for a full twenty seconds, surging towards her shadow and away again. Even from below, the tension was plain in her arms and outspread fingers. She might have been beseeching somebody, or preparing to enter the darkness.

The shambles of Appleby's Big Top is somewhat redeemed by the strangely individual performance of Clara the Swallow, who clearly has a pretty head for heights. Not content with upending herself on a twenty-foot pole . . .

She descended fast. She barely waited for our thin applause, but flashed the same cursory smile over our heads, slipped into her high heels and made for the exit. She was clearly not interested in us at all.

Soon afterwards came the grand finale procession, and it betrayed how few people the circus employed: a mere sixteen. I wondered whether to centre my article on this ingenious use of personnel. I jotted down a few ideas by the light of the mobile box office. Or should I put in a disgusted plea for the animals? Or go into the precarious circus finances?

A few children were being taken round the animal tents in the dark. I found the ringmaster forking hay for the ponies. Showbusiness clung about him like stale sweat. He was wearing a black toupee, which was edged by drifts of greying hair. I tried: 'Mr Appleby?' although the sunny name did not suit him.

His hands lifted to the wax tips of his moustache. 'Uh-huh.'

25

'I'm Features Editor of the *Hampshire Times*. Could I have a word?'

'You want to do something on us?' He left his fork standing in the hay. His moustache was dyed. His skin had a cherry polish. 'Trouble is, by the time the reviews come out, we've already left. What do you want to write?'

'I'm not sure.' A straight review would be too boring. 'Perhaps I should mention the difficulties.'

'You could write a book about those.' Sad lines wobbled down to his mouth across the cherry patina. He said: 'You've come at the worst time. June's always a dead month. People are saving up for their holidays. You should see us in the autumn. We'll have picked up by then.'

'It's been a lean year?'

'It hasn't been easy.' He was reluctant to talk about it. 'Ground rents going up all the time. The councils are the worst. And we've had mechanical problems.'

'But you'll be carrying on?'

'Carrying on?' He echoed the words with an odd, jaunty sadness, surprised even by the question. 'We're a family. What else could we do?' He played with the fork-handle again. 'We keep improving.'

'Clara the Swallow was all right.'

'She's one of our high spots. You could do a piece about her.'

'Yes,' I said. Everything else was too depressing.

He gestured to one of the articulated wagons spread among lorries and caravans. 'She's over there.'

It was almost night. I wandered curiously through the mobile village. Its curtained windows made warm, lit rectangles in the dark. Two Alsatians roused themselves at my approach, settled again, and somewhere a heavy animal was bruising a wooden partition with a deep, repetitive thud. The coloured lights above the tent flickered out. This circus must be closer-knit than any real village, I thought – locked in its own hierarchies, its own time-scale, its own marriages. Appleby's wife, I guessed, was the

26

woman with the pugs; the jugglers were clearly married to one another; one of the clowns had eyes for the blonde cowgirl, and Clara was perhaps the strong-man's partner. In this soft night, through the dim-lit caravanserai, the illusion was of happiness. Voices resonated in the thin walls. There were smells of cooking.

When I knocked on Clara's door, it opened on somebody I could not discern. 'Mark Swabey,' I said. '*Hampshire Times.* May I talk with Clara? Mr Appleby . . .'

'If you like.' Her voice was defensive, a little cold.

We were alone in a cluttered room. The wagon's fittings might have belonged to an old-fashioned liner. Dark wood panelling reached halfway up the walls, and tasselled lampshades made quaint, Victorian pools of light. Clara surprised me. I had expected, for some reason, to meet a young girl. Instead I found a twenty-seven-year-old woman, who was not pretty, but fiercely, irregularly beautiful. Her eyes dominated her face in a glittering acreage of grey-green. They seemed to slant sideways, like a bird's. The dark-blue powder on their lids, and the white crescents fanning their corners, lent them a superfluous glamour. It was a high-boned face, gaunt almost, with sculptural cheeks.

She said: 'Sorry about the mess.'

Against one wall her dressing table was littered with greasepaint sticks, and tins of pancake and moisturiser. The turquoise headdress had been discarded on a chair, and her hair combed out in springy waves. On another table lay a pair of satin circus pantaloons, and a sewing machine disgorged an outrageous vermilion bodice with batwing sleeves attached.

She cleared a chair, and sat on the sofa opposite. She wore a plain dressing-gown over her costume. I detected a discrepancy between herself and the innocent vulgarity of her surroundings.

'You're a journalist.' She had a soft, placeless accent. 'What does that involve?'

'Involve?' I laughed. 'I thought I was meant to be interviewing you.'

She smiled back airily. 'Where do we begin?'

I took out my notepad where I had listed some questions. I felt the extraordinary eyes on me. The questions no longer seemed quite suitable. I had created her as a pretty cliché for my article, and now felt confused. 'I'm afraid I don't know anything about the circus, but your act seemed more . . . less routine than the others. I really enjoyed it.' 'Enjoyed' seemed wrong. 'I mean it was inspiring.' The word sounded fatuous, but I left it there.

She said: 'Thanks.' The searchlight eyes went on staring.

I returned to my notepad. 'I was wondering if you come from a circus family?'

'Oh yes, my mother was an acrobat. She worked in four or five different circuses. In Germany she was quite well known. She was called the British Lioness.'

I glanced at her for laughter, but there was none. Her mother was a special preserve, and dead.

'She taught me from the age of six,' she said. 'I was all arms and legs and pigtails. Circus kids get very independent, you know. I was in the ring before I was ten.'

'And your father?'

It was a tactless question, I suppose, but I'd always thought circus families tight-knit. Clara lifted her head — like a drama student correcting deportment — and stared somewhere over my shoulder. 'He came and went.' That was her way (I later realised) at moments of stress. Her voice would take on a distancing monotone, as if disinfecting some cool, white room in her.

I glanced around for evidence of any companion, but the question, as I put it, already seemed superfluous: 'You're not married?' I wondered why I had thought the aerial figure younger or different. Her spotlit arabesque was all of a piece with her: solitary, adult, self-contained.

'There's not much scope for marriage here.' She laughed with a sudden, flushed charm. 'Clowns . . .'

This interview was running off the rails, I thought. *Clara the Swallow, orphaned and beautiful, is married to a high-wire act in the darkness of Appleby's Big Top . . .* Christ. *Clara the Swallow cannot remember her parentage. She was probably sired by Zeus on a passing aerialiste, because her current circus act treats gravity . . .*

'You're never lonely in the circus,' she said suddenly. 'But you get used to looking after yourself.'

'You even make your own clothes?' My eyes strayed to the bodice.

'Of course.' She let out her cool laugh. 'Where could we ever buy them?'

I fingered the batwing sleeves. 'I suppose these sequins make the costume stand out?'

'That's right. Everything has to be emphasised.' Now she was enjoying some private joke of her own. Her lips curled over closed teeth. 'You don't like these clothes, do you?'

I burst into laughter. 'Well . . . Are you planning Clara the Bat?'

'Those are just to amuse the crowd,' she said. 'They like to see you come on dressed as something silly. I used to have a swallow costume, but it wore out. Anyway, you leave all that behind on the ground. The important thing is what you climb in.'

'Yes, of course.' I recalled the spangled tights. But she must have taken them off: her ankles showed bare under the dressing-gown.

She said: 'The costume should be a bit loose across the diaphragm, otherwise you can't breathe. And free under the arms.' She parted her dressing-gown above the turquoise bodice: breasts nestled in sequins. It was a perfectly unselfconscious act, just as an athlete might display her body, as a neuter instrument. 'The materials ought to pick up the light.' She noticed I was writing none of this down. 'Perhaps that doesn't seem important. Other people go to work wearing what they want.'

'I never think about it.'

29

'That must be marvellous.' She closed the dressing-gown. 'To be able to concentrate on something outside yourself, without thinking: "Am I too this? Am I too that?"' She opened and closed her shoulders.

So it was as I'd thought. The costume and the spectators were irrelevant. They were simply the ambience in which she enacted her aerial dance. Her own taste was impossible to gauge. Almost everything around her looked inherited: the fustian caravan, the flashy clothes. Only the dressing-gown seemed her own, and some glazed pottery animals on a shelf. She followed my gaze: 'You can't own things, living like this. You concentrate on what you do. I prefer that.'

'So do I.'

She said: 'Do you choose what you want to write?'

'Whenever I can.' I explained a little. Her envy pleased me. It suddenly seemed extraordinary to be selecting my subjects, slanting arguments, taking up attitudes. My line in syndication, and successes in the national press, grew rather wonderful. Clara listened with an odd, burning attention. Perhaps this was the result of her training, I thought. Her powers were concentrated on whatever lay to hand. My own profession, by comparison, seemed full of people in various stages of diffusion, who stared past each other at drinks parties. So this intense gaze of hers was at once flattering and odd. It was enough to convert you to the old theory of optics, I felt – that eyes saw by projecting beams of light.

'And now you're interviewing me again.' I held up my notebook. 'Stop. Tell me about your pole act. Why do you do it? What's it all about?'

She looked puzzled. 'About? I don't know. I just do it. What do you mean: "What's it about?"'

'I mean, what motivates you? It looks dangerous. Is it dangerous?

'A bit. Otherwise there's no point.'

'What do you mean?'

30

'I don't know.' She looked faintly distressed. 'But you have to have some danger, otherwise you're not pushing yourself, you're not doing it properly.'

'So what are you feeling up there?'

She frowned. 'I'll have to think about that.' She said this as if thought, like everything else, must be applied with a serene and exclusive concentration. I imagined special periods of her day set aside for it. *Clara the Swallow could not perform her act this week, due to thought. It is hoped, however, that by next week* . . . I doodled over my pad in frustration.

'You don't take any safety precautions?'

'No. That's more exciting. The crowd like it.'

'I had the impression you weren't much interested in the crowd.'

'Did you?' A pause. 'That's bad. Of course I'm interested. Well . . .' – she laughed in sudden collusion – 'perhaps not very. You see, the spectators don't really know one act from another. You can be straining your guts out up there, and they won't know. One evening the shoulder-perch handle snapped off in my hand, and nobody even noticed. They prefer clowns and animals. If an elephant shits, they scream with laughter. When it stops, they clap. That's what they really like. Don't print that!'

'So you don't do your acts for the crowd?'

'I do the old spots for them, I suppose. You get through those automatically. The body just tells you what to do. Of course you can't afford to lose concentration, but the body knows them.' Her voice warmed. 'But the new acts, the ones you're developing, those are different.'

'Like the arabesque?'

'It's not exactly an arabesque. We call it an angel-pose. Yes, you do those for yourself.'

'Did you choose that movement?'

'Yes.'

'Why?' She frowned again, but I went ferreting, bullying on, trying to pin down a butterfly – to discover whatever was beyond, and then uncover what was beyond that. 'When you adopt that pose, are you thinking anything special? An arabesque doesn't place the arms like that usually, does it?'

'Didn't you like it?'

'Yes of course I did. I thought it rather extraordinary. It looked as if you'd seen something up there.'

Clara the Swallow – I actually wrote this, the same evening, after I had left her – *appears to be locating some airborn nemesis thirty-eight feet above the ring in Appleby's Big Top (perfs: 2.30 & 7.30, weekdays). But in fact she is alone . . .*

4

I can hardly believe I've acted so stupidly. I've been working with stained glass for over eight years now, and although I've had my disappointments, I've never been confronted with anything quite so perplexing as this, and it's entirely my own fault. Everything else about the window has gone so well, although it has involved difficult colour choices, and the Archangel Michael, I have to admit, works rather wonderfully. The scarlet streaks in his glass follow the leading uncannily, so that I don't even have to paint in his vestment folds, and the colour is so strong that he stands out from the browns and reds of paradise while still belonging with them. All this may sound vain, I know, but in my craft the effect depends so much on the glass quality that I sometimes feel its beauty has nothing to do with me, that it just arrived there.

But what can I do about Lucifer? I completed the rest with such ease – that should have warned me – and it seems whole in itself now. I wish he could be omitted. It could stand as a study of the Archangel guarding paradise. I've been tempted to try a combination of black and dark-blue Iridescent, but I don't think this would work here, it would remain too dead.

Mark jokes that I don't understand Satan, that I never entertain him, and that's why I can't finish it; but in fact it's he who doesn't recognise evil, he says it's just a word, and that gives him a kind of courage. He would have started with the Devil, of course, with disruption, because all variety fascinates him. In a way I envy that energy, perhaps I'm jealous of it, I don't know. It takes him away from me. It must be like standing always on the edge of dark, wanting to explore and know everything – as if you could.

Last week we went to the parish church at Ashfield to look at its glass, and there seemed to be a completeness there, even to the graves outside of people buried in that peace. The chancel windows depict the Creation on one side, the Passion on the other, and you don't have to be a Christian to feel moved by the mystery of either. Mark thinks I'm a Papist, but most people wouldn't count me a believer at all. Even when I pray I don't know who I'm praying to, it's more like an act of trust; but this place contained all the certainty we're supposed to have lost. It was impossible to kneel here and not to know that some kind of structure and direction exist.

But Mark couldn't see it at all.

Yesterday we discussed my own work again, and he suggested that Lucifer be beautiful, to tease me. 'That's the only way to get you moving again,' he said. 'You can't face ugliness.'

Just the words of love, I know, but he runs his fingertips over the rest of the window, the paradise, and says it bewitches him, and then I feel I'm the reality he returns to, and that all that questing after articles and interviews is just his pastime. With me he says his circle is complete, as if he can never break away again, although I know he will. It is rather terrible, but sometimes when he's with me, and very close, I feel this panic that in a minute he'll be gone, that he's only on loan to me from somewhere else. Good grief, it does seem silly, I should be grateful for these nights, and of course I am, I am. I do wonder why he loves me. I see him kneeling above me and whispering the words so idiotic anywhere but bed, and if I'm lucky I find my beauty in his eyes (because certainly it's nowhere else). And later I think: when will he notice? But by then he's asleep on me, with his wide forehead and dark eyes, a good-looking man, yes (although he denies it).

34

If I ever marry, I'll insist on two children. Nobody should endure being an only child, and I was fat. My father used to refer to me as 'that girl'; he had wanted a son. I can see now, there was a malaise in both of them, my parents, but it's too late and you remake the world, for yourself this time.

Only dreams bring back the old one. I used to share my dreams with a schoolfriend, who dreamed the same ones, as if there was a communal land of such dreams into which you must have a pass. And the pass was our ugliness. The dreams were full of it. She was defaced by a strawberry mark, and I felt I shared it.

Last week, when Mark was away, I dreamed that a man was making love to me: a handsome man. After a while I held him away and said: 'Can't you see I'm ugly?' Then he repudiated me, and I felt an odd peace.

I have a new idea for Lucifer. I think he should be left as he is: transparent white, a kind of gap. Paradise is flame-coloured. Hell is a gap.

5

I was trying to write a feature on the petty crime which erupts in seaside resorts every summer. It was not what Katherine would have called an 'uplifting' subject, but it was full of small dramas and had curious social roots. At times like these, returning to my flat at night was unsettling. I have never made it comfortable. I treated it as a commando-base for raids on the world outside. And in an hour or two I might go to Katherine.

My week had gone badly. A plan to report on the new by-pass had petered out, and I'd even had to emasculate my article on the circus. The Chief Editor of the *Hampshire Times* fancied himself the Randolph Hearst of the Home Counties (he even knotted his tie halfway down his shirt) and half an hour before we put the paper to bed, he returned my article to me with a memo: *Can't print this unless you cut some of the crap about Clara the Swallow. Have you got the hots for this bird, or what? Sounds to me she's just a bit of crumpet teetering on a pole. So amend.*

Looking at an average edition of the *Times*, I wanted to puke. Even our sports diary was out of date before it was printed. When I joined as Features Editor, I was told that the paper was expanding, that there would be scope for national investigative reporting, coverage of wider issues behind the news, and so on. And I was offered a salary to match. Instead we went on publishing as if our highlights had remained Motor Mart and Farmer's Diary. We were still a provincial newspaper in the worst sense. And now my piece on seasonal crime was drifting into an incoherent

36

collage of guesswork and anecdote, glued together with controversial statistics.

It was Midsummer Day, and still light. I kept gazing out of my window. Across the roofs I could glimpse the oaks fringing Peterhurst green, and amongst them a broken scrawl of pink and amber neon: '... pleb..s Bi. .op' – Appleby's Big Top halfway through its final show. At this moment the elephants would be shambling through their courses, circumambulating the iron stools.

There was the germ of a feature article in the strange trapeze artist. Her performance in my mind, and the Editor's memo, grated against one another. The broken neon glowed across the trees with unresolved business. I felt slightly humiliated. I wondered what I had imagined. It wasn't likely that a minor circus act had ascended into the extraordinary. She was simply a handsome young woman performing her variation on a common trapeze turn. Had I been, in some way, manipulated? But I had delayed returning until the last moment, and now an odd apprehension came fanning up inside me.

This coldness continued as I crossed the park. The mobile box office was closed, but I pinned on my press badge and found a seat, unnoticed. The tent was half-full: a Friday night, and the ring-fence overflowing with children who craned above the boards dangling little pennants blazoned 'Appleby's'. The clowns were hamming through their last turn, clouting one another with buckets and a stepladder, while the children squealed.

In the moment's lull between acts, the tension grew in me like a chill air. I told myself: she's just part of a pantomime, afterwards I'll laugh at it, it has nothing to do with real life – with the Peterhurst by-pass, the crime ratio in seaside resorts, with Katherine or with me. It's just make-believe.

She came on wearing a gaudy tangerine cape, and discarded it in a shower of tinsel. Her smile – impersonal as semaphore – shot straight over her audience. The close-fitting headdress, which pulled back the hair from the stark beauty of her features, seemed to slant back her eyes too, so they shone huge and birdlike in her narrow head. The spotlight picked her up ascending in the dark, her small, tight bottom absurdly spangled. The music dinned. She performed her aerial splits automatically, as if exulting in its ease, smiling into space.

Upright again, she intensified the sway of the platform with rhythmic shifts of her weight. Then she bent down, judging the instant, and unfolded into her handstand. The cymbals shimmered and faded. Poised on its swaying tree, the pale body froze for half a minute. Even the spectators seemed awed. You could have heard a mouse squeak. And suddenly I looked through her eyes, and saw the ring below reeling in a dim saucer, and felt a twinge of fear for her. Then I was back staring up at her and wondering: how does it feel? What is its purpose?

'I must ask you to be silent while Clara the Swallow attempts the most difficult . . .'

In the fading daylight the blue tent canopy looked like a night sky. She was balanced close beneath it on the pole's extension. Three, four, five times the platform lurched through its trajectory. Then she entered the arabesque. The tilt of her head, and the thrust of her hands – not in pleading but in an imperious embrace of the dark – touched the moment with an indefinable heroism. In another person the pose might have seemed sentimental, suggested some companion in the night. But not for her. Her arms stretched towards that emptiness as if she might outface it.

My interpretation, of course, and quite unverifiable. The mystery was in her, and she could not explain it. It was just something she did. It had simply blazed above our heads in the narrow tent. Perhaps, I thought, it had nothing to do with anything at all.

After the show had ended, I wandered backstage in the warm night. In the tent beyond the ring doors stood the clowns' jalopy, and a few masks and headdresses were hung up in an aura of dispersed magic. Under a canopy, even in summer, the elephants were swaying back and forth to restore their circulation. Their titan feet were manacled to duckboards, but they swung their bodies in a slow, demented dance, and their deranged bellows followed me into the encampment, where the only other noise was the purl of a lorry-mounted generator.

When I reached Clara's wagon, my reporter's notebook struck me as ridiculous and I put it back in my pocket. Her curtained windows were brightly lit; her door was opened by Appleby. He was wearing the grass-green tail coat which he sported for the finale.

'Ah,' he said, 'the press.'

'My piece came out yesterday. You probably haven't seen it.' I hoped he hadn't: the only passage of praise had been brutally cut. 'I'm thinking about a general feature article. I'd hoped to see Clara.'

He gestured inside with the nervous arm-jerk which ushered clowns into the ring. Clara and his wife were sitting with the strong-man, nursing little glasses of vermouth. I had intruded on a conference.

Mrs Appleby looked uncomfortable. She began: 'I'm not sure that – '

'It's all right.' Appleby sat down and smoothed his scuffed top hat on his sleeve. 'There's nothing secret, and the press may help us.' His watery eyes swerved over me. Their eyeballs were filigreed in red. 'I should tell you that we always used to buy in an act from abroad – Moroccan or Spanish jugglers. But they're too expensive now. So we've got to extend ourselves.' He added wanly: 'It could be good.'

I nodded. Mrs Appleby broke in: 'It *will* be good,' and after that they seemed to forget that I was there.

They were still dressed for the ring. Under her turban Mrs Appleby's face gleamed fat with blue pin-eyes and lollipop-lady cheeks. She had pencilled in her eyebrow-ends with black curves, but had plucked them away in the centre, so they seemed to enclose her face in inverted commas. 'We'll be even better than before,' she kept saying. 'Even better.'

Appleby's coatsleeves drifted over his knuckles. Inside his top hat, I noticed, he had improvised polystyrene lining as if even his head had shrunk. 'The palomino's starting up asthma again,' he said. 'I noticed it this morning. I'd thought we could develop the rodeo act by September, but not now. No.' He added, sighing at his wife: 'So it all depends on you, my dear, whether you can do a second spot in the first half.'

They were padding out the show, like hack journalists. I sensed that Appleby's 'It all depends on you' had become a conjugal rite. His wife craned down at the pug curled on her lap. 'Can we manage? Can we?' The pug yapped back. 'Yes, of *course* we can.' She balanced a sugared almond on its snout. 'Yip-yip-yip.'

Appleby patted her knee. 'That's my girl.'

She said: 'We'll keep the usual opener, but extend the pugs and poodles football.' She peered into her lap. 'And *who*'ll be playing striker then? Guess who? Yip-yip.' Her dewlaps flapped like a turkey's wattles. But in her cottagey face, I sensed, the pin-eyes were calculating. She turned to Clara: 'And have you decided *your* new spot yet?'

Clara had taken off her feathered headdress, and was shaking her hair free. She said: 'We decided on a shoulder-perch act for the first one. Juggling with the hoops. Barry thinks he can cope.'

The strong-man said: 'Shouldn't be a problem.'

He was a listless blond giant, no longer very young. He spoke with a gravelly lisp. His face was still smeared with the walnut dye of his Hindu fireating trick; it stopped short at his neck like a tidemark.

'Juggling with the hoops.' Appleby's voice turned dreamy. 'It'll be like the old days, then, when Barry held up your mama. Two generations . . . Can you still manage the shoulder-perch, Barry? It's been a while.'

Barry said: 'Can do.' He had the neuter polish of a bodybuilder.

'For the second spot, I'll stick to the pole,' Clara said. 'I'm taking my handstand to the top.' Her chin lifted in the slight, characteristic correction of deportment by which she expressed decision and excluded objections. 'It's time I got on with that act.'

My gaze settled on the delicate line of that chin and curved nose – more hawk's than swallow's – and on the mouth tilted up elvishly at its corners.

Appleby said: 'Then you use the safety belt, my girl. Use the lunge wire.'

Clara said: 'I don't think it helps. It interferes.'

'You listen to the boss.' Mrs Appleby squinted down at her lap. 'Shouldn't she be more careful? Shouldn't she?' A sugared almond appeared. 'Yip-yip-yip.'

Clara finished her glass of vermouth and perched back on her chair-edge, her body braced upright in the turquoise costume. Watching them, I found it incongruous that she should be here at all – with Appleby slouched on his green tails, his words stained by years of ringside hyperbole; with the grotesquely sweetened woman, nannying her pug; and the pantalooned Barry, whose blackened head erupted in yellow curls. And you, I thought, sitting in your turquoise bodice. With your beauty, your brightness, your athleticism, you could have been a ballerina. But instead . . .

'Gawks!' said Mrs Appleby. 'Look at the time.' She rose to her feet and turned to me. 'And what sort of thing will you be writing then?'

I said: 'Perhaps something on the dilemma of the circus,' and paused while the pin-eyes narrowed, 'or how it's overcome . . .'

They trooped away like revellers from a fancy-dress ball, or ghosts returning to their proper century. Mrs Appleby's voice kept squeaking and complaining as her high heels

41

dug into the grass, and her husband fed her a litany of
'Steady does it, my dear.'

Clara closed the door. 'She's cross,' she said. 'She wanted
her poodles to change places with my act. I said no.'

'I don't like her.'

'She runs this circus.'

'Appleby looks finished.'

'Finished.' She sat down on her seat-edge again, and
contemplated the word. 'He never really began. He stepped
into his brother's shoes. Literally. You noticed his clothes?'

'Yes.' So that was why the tail coat overshot.

'He can't organise, and nor can she. His brother used to
do it all, but then saw hard times coming and pulled out.
There was a lot of bad feeling. The rest of us felt abandoned.' Her voice had taken on the serene intensity peculiar to her. She might be saying quite ordinary things, but
often this cool fervour irradiated them. Just like her circus
act. She went on: 'It's been hard ever since. We always
seem to be booking in to the wrong places at the wrong
times. The holiday season's coming up now, for instance,
and all our venues are miles from the coast. That can't be
right . . .' She stopped. 'What do *you* think?'

But I was not thinking anything. I was too distracted by
her sitting there, dressed like a Christmas-tree angel, by
the violet make-up of those disruptive eyes, her creamy
skin encased in tinsel, and by the naturalness with which
she accepted me. Just as other women went to work in
skirts or overalls, I thought, so she sheathed her body in
turquoise and sequins, and like this she walked about her
caravan, handed me a drink, and landed this question at
my feet.

'I think you should get out, Clara,' I heard myself say.
'You're too talented for this circus. It's running itself into
the ground. Can't you go anywhere else?'

She looked grateful. It occurred to me that she had
nobody much to confide in. 'I'd like to do outside work.'

'Well then?'

'There's not much scope. I've sent photographs and videos to the agents, but most of them don't even answer. It's hard to sell yourself in aerial acts. Everybody's doing the same sort of thing.'

'Yours is different.'

'Not enough.' She shook her head. 'Did you like it this evening? I think it's getting boring.'

'It's not boring.' I had my notepad open on my knee, for show, but did not know what to ask her. Nothing seemed relevant. 'I found it poignant.'

She said: 'Poignant is when you fall, isn't it?'

Now I hear her say this with desolate simplicity. She is leaning forward a little, not smiling, and has lifted her head slightly as if to present her profile. Yet I've thought about those words too often, and she may not have said them like this at all. Perhaps she was not even thinking much, or laughing, or teasing me. I'm no longer sure.

I said: 'It changes things, having no safety net. It makes it seem you don't care what happens to you, that the only important thing is the act. Because the act is something to do with death, isn't it?'

She frowned momentarily, then her face crinkled into lines. She was laughing at me. 'I suppose it may be, if that's what you see.'

I started laughing too. 'Anyway what's this new turn? What's a shoulder-perch?'

'Oh, that act. That's not very interesting. The perch is a steel ladder which Barry supports on his shoulder. I climb it and juggle on top with gold hoops. The danger comes if Barry loses concentration or can't steady the ladder upright. But he's very reliable. He's been with the circus all his life. He started doing that spot fifteen years ago with Mama. I was there too, aged twelve. I used to throw up the hoops for her to catch. She seemed wonderful . . .'

They drifted into my eye for a moment: the older woman straining to continue her girlhood, in her girl's sequins, her

43

girl's hair-do; and the child below, dreaming her wonderful.

Clara said: 'Is your father like you, an editor? What do your people do?'

My parents seemed drab beside hers – a surveyor, a housewife – but I told her.

'I think that must be better. It's hard to follow parents. I still don't know if I'm as good as my mother. Barry says I'm better, but he always wants to please, and Appleby can't remember.'

I said: 'And what about this new handstand?'

'Ah, that's the one!' The project switched on a floodlight in her. 'I'll take it up the extra nine feet. That's a real height!' She was exultant. Height in itself, I realised, was an intoxicant to her, the ascent to another stratosphere, the sheer distance of herself above the earth.

'No wonder the Applebys want to harness you!'

'It's not much danger. The pole will swing a foot wider, that's all.' She stood up with her back to me and lifted her arms, assessing the height. 'Another two feet and you've reached the platform.'

She went on tiptoe and stretched to the ceiling, her hands gripping air. Above the low-cut costume, her back shimmered into life in a trembling fretwork of fibres and tendons. She looked impossibly sensitised. Yet she was not soliciting approval for her body, but for this dream of ascent and liberation.

'Just sometimes,' she said, 'when it's humid like tonight, your body goes heavy. You can feel your breathing getting harder as you climb. It's so hot up there.'

'So it's worse in the summer . . .' But I could not hold my attention to what we were saying. Her tiptoe stance – the lift of her calves in their atrocious fishnet tights – was too close in the warm room.

'In the heat you use a lot of rosin . . . need to grip harder to counteract sweating . . . I open up blisters sometimes . . .'

'Blisters?' On this absurd excuse I took her wrist and turned over her hand.

She said: 'It's too hardened.'

It was the only unsightly part of her, but charming, laughable. At the base of her fingers lay a crescent of little yellow pads, like the paws of a bear.

I touched them. 'Clara the Flying Bear. If I'd known about this, I wouldn't have reviewed you.'

'Did you review me?' Her head bent over her open hand. Her hair touched mine.

I fumbled the article from my pocket. It was a travesty of what I had intended. She held it between us. I heard her murmur: ' "... graceful and effortless ..." ' She flushed. 'Oh, thank you!' Then she threw her arms round my neck, and kissed my cheek. She meant, I think, to withdraw. But my hands circled her helplessly and my mouth twisted to hers. Her lips tightened, then softened, opened a little. I saw her eyes flicker.

The language to celebrate physical beauty has gone. (My own trade has helped to kill it.) But Clara's was peculiarly her own. Her body seemed not to flow, but to separate and bloom in its different parts, as if human flesh and blood were infinitely more complex than anyone had supposed. Her acrobat's breasts, shoulders, thighs seemed each to throb with an independent, delicate charge of its own, and elements dormant in other bodies – small nerves and sinews and ligaments – had quickened to life in hers.

After a long time I curled my hands behind her to the hooks of her corslet. She looked at me with a kind of vivid calm. The turquoise sequins loosened round her breasts. She smiled and touched them. Then the costume slid off, all of a piece, and she stood in her pants, her shoulders thrown back. Then she flung her arms round me and lifted her head beside mine. Even naked, she seemed composed. She might have been acting love: not consciously, but thinking: 'This is how you behave when loving.' She seemed older than me now (though she was four years

45

younger), and her passion at once extrovert and self-contained.

Close against the driving cabin, her bedroom was like that in a barge, the mattress fitted flush against the walls on either side, in a cave of warmth and perfume. I was momentarily overswept by the strangeness of this, by her violently made-up eyes, by the odd, contained flood of her feeling. She lay on the coverlet, her thighs half parted. A few circlets of hair strayed from her pants. She seemed flushed, luminous.

I heard myself say: 'I love you.' I sounded like a schoolboy.

She switched off the lamp. In the dark she quivered, pulling down her pants. But I could not tell her feelings. I was too consumed by my own, trying to delay, but unable. Her arms came up as I entered her, and pulled me against her shoulders. Her kisses were in my hair.

Hours later, when I woke, a pale light was leaking under the window. One of my legs was still hooked over hers. She had eased the sheet down to her waist in the humid night, and lay peacefully on her back. I could discern her closed eyes and the valleys of her cheeks. I tried to grasp what had happened. I had told her I loved her, and it had become true. I repeated the words softly, trying them out, and half expected her to answer. Her upturned lips seemed to be smiling.

Later, in a dull hour of dawn, I wondered if I had been hypnotised – by some chance collusion of music and aerial gym, by the powdered enormousness of eyes perhaps, by the alien tinsel, the cave-light of her caravan, even her soft accent. Then I began to drift back towards sleep. Was she an orphan prodigy or just a pretty showgirl? I turned drowsily against her, and fondled her shoulder. The Alsatians were stirring outside, growling at the light. Once, footsteps sounded across the grass, and I thought someone was coming to wake us. I felt guilty. But they faded away, and the silence and light intensified together.

6

Sometimes I think I've never lived any reality but in this cell. My memories float anchorless. I lose conviction that they relate to anything that really happened. Perhaps memories are just events in themselves.

I'd thought that remembrance and pain would fade together. But while my past – our past – becomes confused, her absence remains atrocious. I try to picture her, to find one uncontaminated picture, but I've remembered too much, and they've changed into pictures of memories, not pictures of her. I'm horrified by how few there are. Sometimes I avoid recalling them, in order to preserve them.

Memories obsess us all here. They're all we have. It's like living in the hereafter, in your own sick. People go back over their cases all the time, and back beyond that. They call it 'making sense of my life', as if there were some skeleton of meaning inside that amorphous flesh. And I too, of course, am trying to perform this trick.

We're eaten away by forgetfulness. I'm even frightened that what remains of her to me – some letters and small gifts – have gone. Because out there, things exist only tentatively. From this cell window I can't even see the disused church, only the wall. Space has become meaningless. How far away is Peterhurst? Australia? They don't exist very much.

I understand how the will to live preserves some old people. If I were old, I'd be fading away. I used to be harried by time passing. Katherine would tease me because

47

I even went to the lavatory reading a book. I wanted a hundred lives. Now a single one seems too much.

Time here slows to the eventless crawl in which medieval men restricted themselves to an illuminated manuscript or a theological nicety. People become obsessed by crafts they would never touch outside. In the cell next door to ours, Drinkwater models galleys out of matchsticks. He bribes one of the screws for glue and matches, and uses his week's disposable shaving blade to cut them up. They are wonderful, pathetic things. His cell-mate Brown collects out-of-date magazines, and ransacks them to create collages. He'll slice out a cabinet minister's head and stick it on the bust of an actress or a dog's neck, fit out a skull with dark glasses and cigar, or let a bishop taper away in nonsensical newsprint. So he rubbishes and rearranges the world outside, and the cell walls are covered with his hurt. From time to time, when the screws hit and strip a cell at random, his newspapers are all removed as a fire hazard, and he has to begin again.

Our world dwindles to petty expectations. It's just like boarding school. In those days the prospect of Wednesday sweets or a game of French cricket marked off the future with a happy full-stop. Now we look forward to mutton on Saturdays, or to splurging on cigarettes at the canteen (I've started smoking again), or to a football match on the radio.

And I try to read. We're allowed six books a week but this rule, like most of the others, gets bent. The prison library is stuffed with old thrillers and science fiction, and its warder goes to the county library once a month to put in orders there. So I request books from memory or stray reviews, and receive in return a trickle of history, poetry, psychology. Sometimes I can read for two or three hours without stopping, while Morgan sleeps or listens to his radio. But then some paragraph ignites an idea or a memory, and I find my gaze has blurred on the page, or that I'm scanning it for something of my own. Some books seem haunted by Clara. I devour them as if they were in

48

code, although they are actually about pilgrimage, or Jung or the French Revolution. I doodle notes whose significance palls by next day.

Last night I heard hooting outside my window, and I climbed on the chair to peer out. A tawny owl was perched on the prison wall, just above the razor-wire, drowned in moonlight. So close was it that I heard the faint, hoarse wind in its throat before it hooted – the cry of a revenant. And I couldn't get it out of my head that the bird was Clara. Then it flew away with that eerie silence, leaving me bereft.

Sometimes I feel I'm under the shadow of madness here.

Last night, in my sleep, she was balanced under the circus roof, and as she fell the wings burst from her headdress like great sails bellying-out, so that she was left suspended, the wings wrapped about her like those of seraphim, before she faded away.

In the morning Morgan says: 'You were talking in your sleep.'

'Was I? What about?'

'Can't remember. Load of crap. Play Monopoly, okay?'

The game has become a compulsion for him. His disparate eyes wander the board in glee or dismay. The purchase of Oxford Street for three hundred pounds or the putting up of houses on the Strand diverts and focuses all his past ambition. His pasty hands spend longer than ever shaking the dice. I hold my impatience in (too many cell-mates crack each other's nerves). He mutters: 'Shake a four and I gotcha,' or: 'Praying to Lady Luck for a six . . .', as if chance, in the end, were at the root of everything.

At other times, with Monopoly put away, he will start every other sentence with: 'When I get outa here . . .' – and the visions pile up. Then I become irritable, and suspect these years will be his last time of happiness before he emerges to face the wider prison outside. But we have to live on something. I thought Morgan had a wife and family waiting for him, but he doesn't. He has an empty flat in

Cricklewood. In the snapshot above his bunk, where he and his weasel partner celebrate with a middle-aged blonde and a younger man, I had imagined a wife and son. But no, he says. 'Them's clients.'

'Clients?'

'Yup.' They turn out to be his biggest success: a family who parted with twelve thousand pounds before a day's work had begun. Morgan looks at them with affection. 'She was a good sort,' he says, 'gave me a meal every time I went round to estimate. Nicely off too, house full of silver. But I never took anything. I wouldn't do that. I don't hold with that sort of thing.'

Morgan sees himself bifocally and accepts, almost, the honest man his snapshot proposes. After all, respectable people have believed in this man. Morgan simply seceded from him for a while, he feels, under hardship. He will one day go back.

But nowadays the only person he cons is himself. And perhaps not even that. I sometimes think he doesn't want to leave at all. He wants to go on looking through the cardboard shutters of his painted daydream on our cell wall. 'When I get outa here I'm quitting the repairs business. Dolling up flats is the game now. You get a partly rented house on the cheap, then buy out the tenants . . .'

After our doors are unlocked for lunch, Drinkwater and Brown sidle in. They think they're classier than the other prisoners. The con-men do. They settle lugubriously on our bunks, and haggle with Morgan for dope.

Brown is a shambling, blank-faced twenty-eight-year-old, but looks much older. His clouded eyes hunt our cell for magazines to furnish his collages. He's inside for embezzlement, but in the tundra of his face a tiny, cusped mouth habitually insists on his innocence – a story to which no one listens any longer.

Drinkwater asks: 'Got a skoofer, Morgan?' He's almost fifty, small and pert, like a jockey.

Morgan says: 'Quarter ounce of black Pak. That do you?'

50

Drinkwater goes to guard the door, while Morgan picks a battery out of his transistor, which goes on playing. He pulls off the battery's silver cap, and the dark grains trickle onto his palm. 'How's that for electricity?'

I find myself ogling those specks of oblivion. I used to smoke a few careless joints outside, but now that I crave them, they frighten me. In this place you can never know how much self-control remains to you, because control is imposed from outside. So my touchstone is this: I won't smoke that stuff.

Drinkwater says suddenly: 'Lorrimer's coming.'

Morgan starts to tip the hash onto a square of paper, leering at it, wheezing a little. His fist closes over the battery. Then Lorrimer fills the cell. His olive skin is dark with stubble. He looks huge, coldly obsessive. But he is only hunting for dope. 'I see you've opened shop, old chuck. What's the rate?'

Morgan looks up at him. 'You owe me two quid.'

'That's right, I do.' He is humouring Morgan; he emanates contempt. The others sit silent on the bunks, Brown fingering Morgan's copy of *The Star*. Lorrimer points to the hash. 'What d'you want for that?'

'Cost you eight nicker.' Morgan's mouth shuffles wetly over his teeth. 'Plus the other two.'

'You putting the squeeze on me?'

Morgan says: 'I'm doing you a favour, Lorrie. I charge you the regular. Don't like the stuff resold dear, when I sell regular.'

'Who says I resell?' Lorrimer's fists are clenched at his side. 'Here's your eight.' He reaches to the pouch under his shirt. 'And the other two'll come.'

Morgan's face seems to have wobbled out of focus. Slowly his hand withdraws from the square of paper. 'There.'

Lorrimer takes it. 'If I resell, it doesn't stick your arse in a sling, does it?' His stare savages the rest of us. 'I need cash for the out.'

Morgan starts: 'All this eyewash about getting out . . .'

But Lorrimer has gone.

In the silence that follows him, Brown stops flicking over the magazine and just stares at his hands, while Morgan empties another battery onto another paper square. He breathes: 'Bullshitter.' But his hands tremble slightly.

Brown is either retarded or cunning, I can't decide. His life has become one long wail of appeal, in the courts, in the cells. 'I don't figure that bloke, do you? He says it's shit out there, yet he wants to escape.'

Morgan says: 'He's doing life.'

'They'll find him before he's even started, won't they?' Brown is slouched forward, as if he were ill. 'I reckon he doesn't stand a chance. And if he goes on blathering like that, somebody'll shop him.' His cloudy eyes settle on me, expressionless.

'They all talk like that on the fours,' Morgan says.

Drinkwater leaves his station at the cell door and pockets his hash. 'What's Lorrimer got out there anyway? His girl left him, didn't she?' He sits on my bunk, swinging his short legs like a boy, then raps my knee. 'What'll you go back to, guv? Got a family?'

Morgan says: 'Mark here's got a proper ritzy girl. I seen her in the visitors' room.' His wayward eye winks at me. 'Beautiful lady, real domestic-looking: kinda lady I'm gonna get me. Bet she's a good cook. She a good cook?'

I've had to answer these questions before. Morgan has co-opted Katherine into his dream of the outside world. She has become the promise of its womanhood.

'I got my wife too,' says Drinkwater. 'Great lass, been waiting two years already, one to go. My kids, they're all on the up now. Son's started in the garage trade, and it's looking good. Maybe he'll sign up his dad when I get out.' He laughs, and suddenly I can't remember when I heard anybody laugh here before. It echoes like a flat joke. Even the walls refuse it, bounce it back.

I once saw Drinkwater's family visit him. They were

52

seated round the table beside mine. His wife looked bored and sluttish, and the son drawled on purposefully, arrogantly, about his successful business, as if he were engaged in some obscure revenge on his father. Drinkwater just murmured things. Once I heard the youth answer: 'You're living in cloud cuckoo, Dad.' And they left before their time was up.

But he's perky now. His legs go swinging on under my bunk, and he taps my knee for emphasis. 'What I've learnt is you pay your debts in life. You make a mistake, so you pony up, and that's like it should be. Right, Morgan?'

'Right.'

'I admit, I made mistakes. But when you've done your time, you're all square. You're as good as new. That's how I see it. Right, Morgan?' It's impossible to know how sincere he is. His small, overhung eyes dart from Brown to Morgan to me with a jaunty slyness. 'But Lorrimer's welching. He thinks he can just get out, as if he'd never nearly killed a cop.'

Morgan says: 'He's just putting on the dog.'

Brown looks blank. 'Yeah. Right.'

In fact we all know that Lorrimer means it. But it comforts them to pretend he doesn't. In law they're better men than him, they've committed lesser crimes, and will pay less. But he comes into the cell like a black wind, and they all feel reduced. Already they seem finished: even Brown, who is young. In a year or two they will disappear into the fringes of respectable society, into a little of its comfort, and go straight, or nearly. But Lorrimer belongs somewhere else. He burns with this self-belief, perched above some abyss of his own. The difference between him and them is more absolute than that between criminality and innocence.

'Lunch queue started ten minutes ago!' The screw stands angry in our cell doorway. 'You on hunger-strike or what? Move, then.'

Lunch is a waterlogged curry, which I try to work off in

the exercise yard two hours later. Now that exercise is no longer compulsory, hardly anyone takes it. The volunteers are let out together from all three landings, and circumambulate the concrete path, maximum three abreast. I walk here gratefully, where nothing clangs or echoes. I watch the grass and the laurel bushes. They seem contaminated by being grown within our walls, and I imagine them more faded than laurel and grass outside. There is a camellia bush too, and I long for its flowers. Will they be white or pink? A few pointed buds have begun, but there is no telling.

Two prisoners move up beside me. One is Lorrimer, who never does anything without a purpose. The other is his cell-mate Scotty, a thin-lipped Aberdeen man whose trousers bear the fluorescent stripe of a failed escapee. This is the time when the screws note who is associating with whom, and I imagine I'm being used.

Lorrimer says: 'You got yourself a crowd of nonces round your cell, haven't you? Morgan, Drinkpiss and the squawker.'

'They've come from the Scrubs and Wandsworth.' I'm wondering what he wants. 'They've only got a few years left to do between them. They're just waiting.'

'They can afford to.' His frustration burns the air in front of us. We have to keep distance from the preceding group, so his stride tenses to a stamping on the concrete. 'You're let out when you're useless.'

'You'll be out before that.'

'Me? I won't get probation for another nineteen fucking years. And probably not then.'

I hunt for anything to say, but it's like consoling somebody for their own death. I can barely find a cliché. In the end I start: 'You could study in here for something, engineering . . .'

Lorrimer explodes soundlessly. But I hear it. He says: 'Study engineering, for Chrissake! Do a six-month Vocational Training Course so I can mend some bastard's

54

carburettor in twenty years' time? Fucking hell, Swabey, when were you born?' He turns on me. His face is filled with his dementia. His fingers jab at his eyes. 'Look at me! I'm not Morgan. I'm *young*. By the time I get out of this nick I'll be finished! What kinda berk stays anywhere for twenty years? Would you? *Would you?'*

I can't answer. It's as if he's a part of myself I've lost. Escape has no meaning for me.

He goes on: 'What do they want you to do in here? *Stitch mail bags!* I'm let into that Portacabin gym once a week, and start training, then I look at my body and think; Jesus, what's the point? What's this chassis gonna look like in twenty years?'

'You'll be forty-four. That's not old.' But even to me I sound weak, passive, and I disbelieve myself.

'Forty-four! What sort of schlubette's gonna want me then? D'you think I'm gonna wait twenty years? I'll go mad. I even lech after that ragged-out probation woman that comes in Fridays. I've got a *life* in me. Nothing's gonna keep me.'

Scotty says in a clipped, dry voice: 'Plot it right, you'll make it.' Then he goes back inside, leaving Lorrimer and me to pace round the whitened walls, the laurels, the camellia, and I'm still not sure what he wants.

He says: 'It's no sweat for you. You just got a few months left, that right?' There is a silence before he adds: 'I heard you worked in the circus.'

'Not really. I was a journalist.'

'Uhuh. I remember.' His stride has relaxed. 'Didn't you kill your moll?'

I've swivelled round. My fists are clenched in his pull-over. Its PD label quivers at his neck. His eyes have widened. *'Don't ever say that again!'*

He pulls down my wrists. 'Screws coming.'

'You – you – ' – the screw can't remember my name – 'you want to be stuck on a charge? What's your name?' He's short and elderly. Bald patches show under his cap, where the hair has fallen out, leaving tufts. The screw behind is speaking into a walkie-talkie.

Lorrimer says: 'Mark here was just joshing. Christ, can't a bloke josh around?'

'That right?' The screw walks between us. He stares at me. 'That right?'

Suddenly I realise that the thought of losing remission, of spending any longer in this place, appalls me. Obscurely I think: so I'm alive after all. I say: 'That's right.'

The concrete path is jammed with prisoners. The screws go back to their station by the wall, arms akimbo. At moments like this I realise how frightened they are. We go on walking, and the crowd loosens and unfurls behind us.

But Lorrimer says: 'I remember now, it was in the papers.' He touches my shoulder. 'Sorry, mate.' We pass the screws in silence. 'I remember her picture. She looked a smasher.'

It is the first time that anybody has spoken of her since I came here. I feel as if I am breathing from some sealed part of my body: deeper, warmer. 'Yes, she was.' Strange to hear her praised, as if she lived again. My monthly visitors have no language for her. They only speak of the present, or the future.

I find myself saying: 'Thanks, Lorrimer. I'm still tensed up. You may have saved me some time there.'

'No sweat.'

But I think of his twenty years, and feel ashamed.

7

Kathering looked like Morgan's ideal that day. Under her wide-brimmed hat her face wore its look of quiet plenitude, and she was dressed in her raspberry-coloured suit and matching shoes.

The church was squat and wide-aisled. Its congregation filled the pews beside the north transept while the priest stood at its improvised altar. Above him Katherine's window hung behind a twenty-foot curtain, and her hands twisted together because she was unsure of its solution, and because all this attention secretly dismayed her.

Other windows shone calm with their sunlight. In one, some fragments of medieval glass had been reassembled, and glowed in broken coats-of-arms: mitres, casques, helms. A choir sang reedily from the chancel. The organ throbbed. In front of us, the widow who had commissioned the window sat among whispering friends and parishioners, and the priest smiled at them.

My mother, who was fond of Katherine, stood on my other side. It was over fifteen years since we had stood together in church, and I was shocked by how small she was. I looked down on a greying head a foot below me, and her fingers, dappled by liver spots, wandered over the hymn-book page. Emphysema stopped her singing. Even the prayers came from her in wheezing clauses. I had grown at once protective of her, and impatient. Asthma, bronchitis, emphysema – no attention from husband or sons had ever quite freed us from the blackmail of her illnesses. But she was bewildered by the successive blows which fell on her, and her most effective weapon – self-accusation – was wielded unconsciously. 'I know I'm just a nuisance to you all . . .'

Now, O Lord, we dedicate this window to Thy glory . . .

Its curtain slid back. For a second the congregation stared up as one person, then splintered into chirruping heads.

My mother leaned forward and patted Katherine's knee. 'It's wonderful,' she said. 'You're a wonderfully clever girl.'

The vicar seemed to have a flair for theatre. The organ breathed softly while he read from Isaiah. *The whole earth is at rest: they break forth into singing* . . . The triple window burnt above us. In the conflagration of its colours, the intricate ammonite of the godhead, lodged high under the arch, seemed to be shedding down a rain of jewels, down through the nursery of the blessed, down through the paradise orchard, through the meadows of crimson and copper and ruby, until they almost clattered on the transept floor.

Hell from beneath is moved for thee to meet thee at thy coming: it stirreth up the dead for thee . . .

In Lucifer Katherine had achieved a subtle triumph. In the end she had given him no colour at all, but had transformed his body in opalescent glass, frosted (she later told me) by acid and soda crystals. Now, twisted in the slipstream of the leading, he divided paradise like an icicle, and plummeted to Hell in a white aureole of his own.

I realised again how skilful she had been with the whole composition. As the panes moved upward, they grew gradually smaller until they were swept into the intricate whorls of the Creator. But the rays which streamed downwards, unifying the whole window, had been scored with thin sticklights which caught the sun. Their brilliant order shone through Eden.

The congregation pointed and murmured all through Isaiah. But I felt them like a violation. The window had opened to all of us the territory of Katherine's thoughts. She had refused to create ugliness. In Lucifer, above all, she had committed a radiant blasphemy. The creature was beautiful. It fled from heaven in an androgynous whiteness of face and wings, more angel than demon.

How art thou fallen from heaven, O Lucifer, son of the morning! For thou hast said in thine heart, I will ascend into heaven, I will exalt my throne above the stars of God . . .

I squeezed her arm and murmured praise. I felt her pleasure, without looking at her. Yet she was longing to go home. My mother spoke in my ear, but her voice was so breathless and soft that she might have whispered it: 'Look at the marvellous babies.'

They were not babies. They were the swaddled souls of the dead. But their innocence was quaintly comforting, and the children leading the calves and lion cubs through the gardens below might have been climbing to them. Gentled perhaps by my mother's depletion, by the throb of the organ, by the hymn, I entered the landscape of Katherine's mind. It engulfed me like homesickness. And I cherished her for this: for her peace, her unshared faith. In these few minutes my love for her seemed vested with a natural rightness. More deeply than anything, I wanted to love her exclusively, and I pushed Clara out of mental sight, and even believed her gone.

Katherine seemed to sense my emotion (she usually did), peered up from under her hat, and shifted her feet on the flagstones. I wanted to put my arm round her. I don't know what I was protecting her from. But instead I kept my eyes on the stippled trees of her paradise, where the wolves and lambs were still united in the vitrified sun.

My mother's eyes were watering. She closed her hymn-book.

I am with her in another early garden. She cannot run because of her asthma, but as a boy I pull her along the herbaceous border, whose few yards stretch to a child's infinity, and she nicknames the plants: lamb's tail, monkshood, catmint . . .

And the strangeness is that nothing happens. My earliest memory is eventless, carries no tension, let alone trauma. We simply watch the buddleia in the sun, weighted down with butterflies. I hear my child's voice pipe: 'Just *look* at them all!' and the buddleia sways under their weight: Tortoiseshells, Red Admirals, Peacocks, a Purple Emperor. We are waiting for the Monarch butterfly, which does not come. But the sun drenches the rest, and my mother is standing there, sufficient, and the buddleia swaying . . .

Katherine said: 'Thank God that's over.'

But it wasn't. We were invited to the vicarage for coffee, and the vicar introduced her as 'a lovely old-fashioned girl', which made her wince, and two parishioners complimented her on the babies. But the widow who had commissioned the work – a dignified woman in late middle-age – took her by the arm and said the window was finer, more striking, than she could ever have hoped.

Eventually Katherine took refuge with me. She was hesitantly pleased. My mother watched us with her look of odd, plaintive sharpness. I had the impression that she was willing our wedding (our 'settling', she would have said) before the last of her health deserted her. But perhaps this was only my imagination; and Katherine, who was estranged from her own parents, talked with her about hydrangeas rather than face the brittle, guileless chatter all around.

'I think we can go now, can't we?' She took my arm. 'It's nearly one o'clock.'

We slipped back into the church. Her glass floated in shadows. In our absence, I felt, it had been involved in some life of its own. Katherine was full of small dissatisfactions: a speck of pigment flaked away by firing, a vestment too lightly stained. I said: 'Only you would notice those things. Everybody thought it magnificent.'

'Did they?' She turned and buried her face in my chest.

Her arms crept under mine to hold me. 'Provided *you* think it's all right, then it's all right.'

At such moments she seemed to be immolating herself in me, extinguishing her own worth, which all at once she did not believe in. I fondled her hair. 'It's superb.' I teased her: 'It would stay superb even if I'd never seen it!'

Her voice suffocated against me. 'I'm just glad you like it.'

At these times she seemed to discover her value, her existence, only in my love, and this self-dissolution paradoxically took her away from me. It touched me with alarm. She became a part of me, and so I lost her. I think I felt this more sharply now because of Clara, who existed so fiercely in her own certainty.

Katherine said: 'It may be all right.'

I went on fondling her hair with an irritated sadness. Over her shoulder, the window darkened and lit as clouds scraped the sun outside. As I gazed at it, I tried to relive its earlier power. But it seemed less embracing now. Perhaps it was the absence of that collusive organ, or of the congregation's faith, but the window appeared to hang farther away, as if it were subtly irrelevant.

I don't understand this man holding Katherine. He had not confessed Clara to her. Instead he waited dumbly for some resolution, as if the knot would unravel of its own accord. Perhaps these two women, their two spheres, were so disparate that he could entertain them schizophrenically, without collision. Prisoner 63176 finds it hard to remember.

I ask Morgan: 'Did you find a con-man's life easy?'

He says: 'Gets a habit.'

But I think of holding Katherine, and knowing – I must have known – how I would soon wound her, and I wonder how I took her future suffering so easily, as if I had never suffered myself. Because I had. I had undergone my father's death and, long before that, the lesser deaths that

61

nobody escapes. Dry leaves under rhododendron bushes still make me sick, bushes not thick enough to hide me at school, where a prefect kicks me in the groin, and my best friend Simpson says 'Here, Swabey, drink some of my tea,' and pisses into my mouth. Suppurating there, under the autumn leaves, under the crimson and copper, her paradise . . .

'I suppose we should make a move.' I pressed her back from me. She smiled sleepily.

'I'm still not happy about that stain firing . . .' She went on finding tiny faults, while I reassured her. The sun had clouded over and I thought perhaps this was why the work had died on me. But then the light returned and still something seemed to be missing, and I could not define it. While Katherine worried over details, I became uncertain about the whole. It was beautiful, of course, and in its way complete. But it struck me as stagnant now. It encompassed everything – sin, faith, damnation, paradise – yet related to nothing at all. I tried to shake myself free of this, to indulge my eye in its colours, but could not.

8

When they told me the name, it meant nothing. I thought Mr Jefferson must either belong to my lawyer's chambers or be a journalist hunting a story (the press-box at my trial had been full of them).

The prison visitors' room, in any case, carries a peculiar charge of distress. We wait at our tables like schoolboys anticipating a treat. But it is not a treat for the visitors, who trickle through the glass doorway after being searched. They look soured by worry or tense with embarrassment.

But suddenly the world is full of women. There seem to be so many that as each appears in the doorframe I am haunted by the expectation − insane but irrepressible − that somewhere amongst them, any moment, turning the passage corner, she will be there. But I see my agony in the looks which visitors cast me, and deflect my stare to the duty officers at their desk, and compose my expression.

The instant Jefferson appears, I realise. He lumbers like an ox between the tables: Barry, the strong man. I feel moved and nervous. He wears a brown suit, long outgrown and buttoned up in front. His chest and shoulders stretch it out of true. Among all the faces here − jaded, disconsolate, corrupted − his carries a farmyard innocence. He overflows the chair in front of me. 'Circus come to town,' he says. 'I remembered you was here.'

Clara used to show me circus photographs from as long as fifteen years ago, and Barry was often in them. Rock-like and melancholy, he would be supporting her mother on one shoulder or upraised palm, or tossing Clara herself − a twelve-year-old elf − like a beach-ball into the air. Now he places his huge, hairless hands on the table-top, and smiles.

For a while the shiny suit dissociates him from any memories – he might have blundered in from a Scandinavian village – and this confuses and relieves me. But then I notice, under his fingernails, the walnut dye from his Hindu fire act, and within a minute he is exuding that heady, enclosed world.

It had been like entering a secret. The moment Clara reached up for one of her turquoise costumes – she always held it against her body as if something might have changed – this private magic began. In the cold striplight above her dressing-table, she would heighten the colour of her lips or cheekbones, and open out her eyes with gentian greasepaint, while watching herself in vivid self-appraisal. While she took in this transformed person, her mind went ahead of her, and her voice would grow faintly more formal. My intimacy with this ritual never quite dissolved its strangeness. As each layer of her disguise completed itself, I had the impression that she subtly withdrew, that the touching up of her skin with moisturiser, or the drawing of a cherry line along her lips, dropped a tiny gauze between us.

I loved and was jealous of this actress she became.

In the ringside tent, just behind its curtains, she would spend a few minutes exercising: touching her toes, circling her arms, running on the spot; then she would turn to me, irradiated by excitement, by her body's confidence, and cup my cheeks in her fingers with her sudden, formal tenderness, and kiss me.

'Next year I'm going to start the flying trapeze,' she said. 'I'm going to end up doing a triple.' She touched my neck with her premeditated gentleness. We could hear the clowns outside, biffing each other for the last time. I had no idea what a triple was. But it evidently didn't include me. I said: 'So you'll have no time for anyone.'

But her eyes had refocused. Her hand fell away. I thought she had seen somebody over my shoulder, and she had. It was herself, in the full-length mirror by the entrace. She said: 'I must go in now.'

For a minute she corrected herself in the glass. She did this every time before entering the ring or leaving the tent. She would settle her shoulders and the tilt of her head, unsmiling, then put on her cape and smooth the blue feathers above her ears. The man behind her was loitering uncomfortably. I was not used to adjusting him in any mirror, and he looked gauche there. I realised then how her looking-glass self had poised and possessed her. She surveyed this self professionally, without vanity. I said: 'You look fine,' but she did not hear. She had gone away into this projected Clara – the exquisite exterior which was, for all I know, her essence, more important to her, more total, then any other self. A moment later she had vanished through the curtains.

Soon afterwards I dreamed strangely of her. I was walking inside a temple, displaced in time. As I approached its statue, I saw that this was one of those precious, composite ones known only from history: a slant-eyed goddess. It was formed of many gold and ivory parts, but it had no unifying essence at all. The idea of selfhood, it seemed to say, was a pathetic romanticism. There were simply these glittering parts. And when I touched them, they fell away in my hands.

Barry shifts uncertainly in the prison chair. He looks abashed, as if it constitutes betrayal, when he says: 'Got a new perch act going. It's not the same, though. Australian girl, very strong. But it's not like Clara.'

I say painfully: 'Do they talk about her still? The Applebys and the rest?'

Slowly he shakes his yellow curls. 'You know the circus.

Always something to be doing. Not much time for remembering.'

'I know.' She would have condoned that, I think. She used to say it was pointless looking back. She would not have approved my grief.

She always took our loving more naturally than I did. The language of the body came more easily to her. Yet that lingering aura of theatre, the unconscious self-discipline which corrected the line of her head and shoulders – and perhaps heart – sometimes confused me, as if the woman in my arms had been invaded by the Clara of the looking-glass.

But of course I was in love with both. After the last evening show, we would sometimes come together so urgently that only the trashy tights and the stiff lower part of her costume would peel off before we lay together, she in her turquoise feathers, exotic, laughing: and for a moment I would feel that I had compassed this paradise-bird, her aerial dance, and everything important.

Often I would motor two hundred miles in the evening to be with her. I would come upon the circus nested like a wagon-train in the circle of its lights, camped out on soggy greens or farmers' rented fields. Sometimes it was still light, and I would be in time to see the elephants shamble through their paces (I had grown fond of them) and would catch Clara tripping to her performance through the slush with her high-heeled shoes in her hands.

Once the circus settled close to Peterhurst, and I brought her back to my flat for a morning. She wore her look of poised containment, I remember, dressed in jeans and a loose blouse. But her eyes and swept-back hair gave her the aura of a nomad who has strayed into an office. The urban rootedness all around stirred up some wildness in her. She could not keep still. She fingered through all my records, then my books. What was this about, what was that about, how did I rate this . . .?

'You've got so much,' she said, without envy. 'I know

it's not really much, but when I compare . . .' She prowled about, looking through the different windows, as if one of them might frame something extraordinary. Then she picked among my books again: 'All that knowledge!', turning to fondle my head. 'And nearly all *useless,*' laughing.

Momentarily I had become as exotic to her as she was to me. The few superfluous things she owned − her pottery animals, gilt-framed photographs, paperbacks − had to be stacked away each Sunday evening, and every surface swept clear, before the circus moved on. Most of her possessions stayed permanently in drawers and boxes, where I discovered them piecemeal: cassettes of popular classics, circus memoirs, childhood toys.

Suddenly she said: 'I must seem very stupid to you.' She spoke it with quiet curiosity, as if my love was starting to mystify her.

'Stupid? *You? Since when?'

She said: 'I'm not educated.'

'What's that got to do with it?'

Even when declaring her ignorance, she appeared invulnerable, as if her completeness lay elsewhere. 'We never went to school enough. We used to go to local schools wherever the circus was, and sometimes they just got missed out.' She stared at the council houses from my back window. 'The other kids seemed right snobs. They wondered how we could bear to live in caravans, and we wondered how they could bear their semi-detacheds. That was half our conversation: "But how can you *bear . . .?"'

'They probably envied you.'

'They were amazed by us, I think. We were bright in a way. We'd already been out in the ring, you see − I did a race with an emu over hurdles − and we were much more *extrovert.* Is that a word?' she laughed. 'School seemed pointless.'

I imagined her existing already in the confidence of her body, perfecting the looking-glass Clara; whereas I − I would have been one of the urban kids, lumbering behind her, socks down and satchel askew. I would have had a crush on her.

As she stared through the window and I watched her restlessness, her delicate hawk's profile, I realised with dulled astonishment that I wanted to marry her. The recognition came quite naturally, unbidden. With other women, with Katherine, the question of marriage had torn me with inner debate. But with Clara any decision was lifted out of my hands. I had no choice. Against this restful miracle, the fact that she was wedded to the circus, and that the circus excluded me, seemed unimportant. There would come a natural time for us, I thought. I would know the moment.

I heard myself say: 'If you got a better offer than Appleby's, you'd take it, wouldn't you?'

'Yes, of course.' The huge eyes turned on me, but saw nothing I meant. She started pacing round the room again. 'But I don't think I could leave them for good. They're like family. I couldn't let Appleby down.'

No, I thought, the old man was all she had for a father. 'If you – '

'Oh look!' She alighted on a file full of my articles, and began to pore over them with mischief and fascination. Since I had met her, my work – it seemed to me – had taken in more varied points of view than before. It was less enclosed, less frowning. I attributed this to her. Because she never sat in judgement. She was simply fascinated or repulsed by things, by the way they worked, or looked or sounded, and this fervour of response concentrated all her energies. Yet it was paradoxically controlled, protected. Even in bed, she seemed to burn immune.

Clara-the-hawk: why is she inscrutable? (I started inventing articles.) *How does she manage to be both vivid and cold? This is the mystery of her high-wire act. It's a brilliant balance . . .* In my bed that morning, kissing the silk of her shoulders, sleepy, I demanded if she loved me.

She sat up. 'Of course I love you!' Her fingers riffled through my hair and the debilitating eyes stared down.

I said: 'More than the circus?'

She swung her feet onto the floor and pulled on her jeans. She took refuge in the expression which had become a joke between us: 'I'll have to think about that.'

But a minute later, just as we were leaving the bedroom, she noticed the photographic portrait of Katherine on my chest-of-drawers. She looked at it in silence a moment, then asked: 'Is that *her*?'

'Yes.' I had scarcely talked about Katherine to her. Then Clara had listened gravely and had understood (she said) my plea for time. But the weeks had become two months now.

She went on looking at the portrait, then said with faint sadness: 'Is she posh?'

'Not really. A little, I suppose.' (Could you be only a little posh? Posh seemed an absolute.)

Clara said: 'I can't imagine what it's like to be anyone else.' How strange, I thought. 'She's pretty.'

'Yes.'

The face was disturbing her. Perhaps she had never imagined Katherine in person before. That was not the sort of imagining Clara did. But now, confronted by the evidence, she looked resentful.

'What did you say her job was?' Her voice held its calming tone, the tone of laying things to rest, in herself or outside.

'She makes stained glass, mostly for churches.'

'I don't think I've been in a church.'

It was the kind of remark, quite unselfconscious, with which she would suddenly astonish me. Another time she mentioned: 'I've never had a post-card' – and I realised that of course, there was nowhere for one to go. And once she asked me with her pert curiosity: 'What's a dinner party like?'

At such moments the ground between this vibrant,

twenty-seven-year-old woman and myself seemed suddenly to yawn open, and the strangeness of my loving her would break over me. Now I echoed: 'Never been in a church?'

'Only a cremation chapel. My mother was cremated. It'll sound silly, but I don't think I really understand churches.' She looked at me as if I might explain them. She was still holding Katherine's photograph at her waist. 'I can't believe any of that about miracles.'

'Nor can I.'

She replaced the photograph on the chest-of-drawers. She said: 'Mark, I want to be first.'

She filled the schoolgirl sentence with adult intensity. I knew I had been unfair to her. I said: 'You will be, you are first. I promise.'

She wanted everything ordered, straight, open. When I had asked her about her past relationships, she had spoken of them as passions to be contained rather than celebrated. Of Barry she had said only: 'No, I've never had trouble from him. He loved my mother, but she wouldn't look at him . . . or any man after my father went. Barry was too young for her, I suppose, and too old for me. No, I don't think he loves me.'

Now he is revolving his shoulder-blades against the back of the prison chair, frowning, trying to formulate a question. Suddenly he blurts out: 'Did she suffer? In the end, I mean. Did she feel any pain?'

'No,' I say. 'You don't feel anything.'

'Good.' His frown fades. 'That's good.'

I reach out and grasp his arm. Is he the only person left who really remembers her? I stare into his pale blue eyes. They look like shallow water. I say: 'You loved her, didn't you?'

'We all loved her.' I believe he is too guileless to be avoiding my question. He just thinks he is stating a fact. My fingers relax.

*　*　*

He would practise with her for an hour every morning through the late summer. She would mount his back, then climb the twenty-foot steel pole poised on his shoulder. After that, he stood so solid that everyone forgot him. Balanced on the perch, she would juggle with four gold hoops, then slip them round her elbows and wrists and revolve them. She and Barry became so adroit in practising this act that its sheer ease turned it rather lustreless. Their shabby leotards, and the absence of music or spectators, left it unsupported. Clara, in any case, grew bored by it even before its first performance. ('The hoops are just painted cardboard, I want metal ones.')

Sometimes the Applebys settled by the ringside and watched. Without the desperate illusionism of his top hat and tails, Appleby seemed paradoxically incomplete. His jet-black toupee and moustache might have been stuck on by a child defacing a poster. The lines down his cheeks looked like tear-tracks. As for his wife, the circle formed by her shoulders and cradling arms was always closed by a pug. Her hair haloed her face in frizzles. Her tiny, cynical eyes missed nothing. Mr Appleby thinks this, she would announce, or Mr Appleby says that – while he sat quiet beside her, massaging his cheeks. I came close to hating her. She never cared for Clara, although she affected motherliness. She was jealous. Her own daughter – one of the lumpish cowgirls – did an acrobatic turn with horses, and sometimes fell off. It occurred to me too that old Appleby's eyes watered over Clara with a little more than fatherly concern, and he would sometimes squeeze her arm when standing near her, and his hand lingered at her waist.

They needed her drastically. On the first morning that she practised her handstand at forty feet, they sat down beside me to scrutinise. Suddenly Mrs Appleby turned to me and said: 'I hope you won't try to take our Clara away from us?' The words held a dulcet challenge.

'You overestimate me.'

71

The apple cheeks dilated into a smile. 'Well I'm glad I do then. Perhaps I do. The circus has always come first with our Clara.'

Appleby was staring up at the pole which Clara, for the moment, did not allow to sway. 'She's our mainstay,' he said simply, and I felt guilty. 'Look at her there. Just like her mother. Always trying to do that bit extra.'

'That's her nature,' said Mrs Appleby.

'She's extraordinary,' I said.

Mrs Appleby tweaked the pug. 'It's hard work does it. Practice and discipline. It's all hard work.'

Forty feet above us, Clara was bunched forward on her arms, then uncoiled into her handstand as if she were boneless. The practice spotlight stamped the roof with her shadow. I tried to live her experience there: the canvas grazing her feet, the sliver of platform holding nothing but a forearm-brace, and the dizzying drop. She never looked down or called to us. No wonder she faced so naturally the fact of human solitude, I thought. In her aerial exile, returning again and again to the same sequence – balance bunch, unfold – she might have been studying loneliness.

Even in the most unifying moments of our love, this acceptance of mutual solitude remained. It filled me with mixed sadness and respect. Yet she did not even know that she exuded it – it was simply a part of her truthfulness, of her confusing simplicity. She acknowledged a human separateness which I never deeply accepted, and against which Katherine's whole loving was a cry of protest.

Mrs Appleby said: 'I can't make out if her balance is as good as her mother's was.'

'The past always seems rosier.' Appleby puffed out his cheeks with authority. 'I think the daughter's best.'

'Her mother had more experience,' Mrs Appleby said. 'That's only natural.'

Clara had descended to the lower platform now and was practising her arabesque. Even in rehearsal she released it into space with a serene daring. If she had ever analysed her actions or motives, I thought, she might appear less unaccountable. As it was, her extroversion created symbols, acts unaware of their own meaning. Or so it appeared to me. But then anybody – if you concentrated on them enough – reverted a little to the unknown. It was just a by-product of love. Clara did not seem a conundrum to anyone else around her.

I said: 'I hope she'll keep that safety harness on.'

Appleby groaned and rubbed his cheeks. 'She won't listen. She'll always wear the lunge for rehearsal, then refuse it for performance. She's a law unto herself. She did fall in rehearsal once, and she didn't care a bit. We found her dangled in mid-air on the lunge-wire, *laughing*.'

'She wasn't laughing,' Mrs Appleby said. 'She was hysterical.'

'I remember her – laughing.' Appleby had become quite spirited. 'She's a circus girl through and through.' He turned to me. 'You know, the circus has a hypnotic effect on some people, especially girls. Girls who fancy circus men always get sucked in. They never leave.'

But what of men who fell in love with circus girls, I wondered? What would I do if she refused to quit?

I thought: I'd become a freelance journalist and live with her. To desert my sedentary life for hers would be a kind of shriving. The Applebys were right in a way: Clara belonged here. Even her complaints rang like a family squabble rather than an employee's rebellion. I could not imagine anchoring her in another life. It would be like plucking a bird from its forest.

Yet she was, I felt, different from the others, maturer. Circus people seemed not quite grown up. They carried an aura of make-believe, of suspended childhood. Even when old, like the Applebys, they resembled broken dolls. But they never gave up. They would go on until they dropped. Sometimes I felt that even an audience was superfluous to them. They did what they did because they had to, and there was nothing else they could do. What rankled was the sheer seediness of this particular circus. But then the *Hampshire Times* was becoming seedy too.

Clara unhitched her belt and descended. We went out into the sun. I asked: 'How was it? Was it all right?'

'I wish they hadn't put the heaters on. The fumes choke you up there.'

We wandered into the elephant tent, where the creatures were swaying in ghostly unison. Their mouths sagged in pink triangles. They looked unquantifiably old. I remember saying: 'I hope you'll keep the lunge for the performance.'

She said: 'Oh that. It gets in the way. And it's a sort of reminder.'

'What of?'

'I suppose of the fact that you . . . weigh something. I just don't need it.' She patted the fumbling trunk of one of the elephants. Its eyes looked out like those of some sad humanoid trapped in its bulk. She said: 'I'd be more likely to fall wearing that lunge . . . Anyway, the crowd don't like it.'

It haunts me that I can't remember what I replied. I would like to think I'd been angry or that I pleaded with her, but I didn't. Instead I knew what she meant. The spotlight always picked out the lunge-wire against the dark. Then the crowd below would be reminded of the artist's limitations, her mortality, and the drama would unfold securely, dead. But without it, a trapeze act was transformed into something perilously living, until at best it transcended the consciousness of danger in artist and spectator together, and became disembodied.

Last week a prison warder returned from the county library with three books I had begged, and I find in one of them this: *Audiences are always cruel. The ancient Romans would not have condoned amphitheatre atrocities in their homes. The element of theatre is crucial.*

In this confinement my memories repeat and distort themselves chronically. I wonder now if Clara's fierce independence arose from her father's desertion, but when I ask Barry this it seems beyond him. 'That man,' he says, 'Clara never knew him. He was brought in from another circus for a season. Used to train horses.' That was twenty-nine years ago, and his knuckles still grind on the table-top.

Even to me, it was baffling that I loved two women so different. Katherine, beneath her calm, opened up a whole sea of feeling, where I sometimes went in fear of drowning. She felt, in my arms, that she simply became my love, that she did not separately exist, and she called this self-dissolution unity. This closeness, for her, was an end in itself, perhaps the greatest. Then she seemed to be inhabiting her own paradise, and my desire for her would turn to protective tenderness. With her I felt mature, and in some way finished, home. And the world shrank, as if she had sucked its importance back inside her.

'You only have to note people's eyes,' Morgan tells me – he says con-men should never blink – and in this cell, in my need, such platitudes take on oracular depth. Katherine's eyes promote her look of a Murillo madonna; they are luminous, introverted (and now suffering).

Clara's were brilliant and afflicting; she resembled, of course, a species of unearthly bird (the circus got that right). We seemed to make love under an open sky, and the outside world kept its possibility. Yet perversely I hankered for the yielding of that diamond clarity. With her I felt younger than I was, vitalised, but reaching always for something withheld.

Perhaps, in the end, the difference rose from power: that I held Katherine in my arms, but Clara held me in hers.

Barry has brought me some sports magazines, and talks about football. But when he looks at me a faint knot gathers between his eyes. In the past he always watched me with this bovine sorrow, and I imagined he was jealous.

But the same look is on his face now, and she is gone. It is a look of compassion.

I know he is my last link with her, and I long for replies to questions it is futile to ask. But I interrupt his thoughts about Manchester United and say: 'Barry, did she ever talk to you about me?'

'Yes she did.' His frown returns. 'Not much. A bit.'

'Did she say anything about our future, or marriage?'

His shoulders shift and strain inside their jacket. The blank candour of his face turns it opaque to me. At last he says with his odd, gravelly lisp: 'Circus people don't marry outside.'

Of course this is not true. But it is the kind of statement Clara might have made. They seem to share a language. I feel momentarily bitterly excluded. So that, I realise, is why Barry always looked at me as he did. He believed that she was married to the darkness under the tent roof, and he was pitying me.

9

You don't grow up until your parents have gone.

Mama and me were driving behind the stalls wagon on the way to Amersham, when our wagon skidded into the kerb and stopped. Have we run out of petrol? I asked, because Mama was leaning down and seemed to be staring at the dashboard. But she didn't answer. I thought: She can't be just going to sit there, without saying goodbye, or warning me. I was nineteen, but it shows what a baby.

About my mother. She was the world to me, because my father was never there at all. I must have modelled myself on her, as Mark would say. But she was more of a woman than me, and for a trapeze artist she was big. Most of us are just five foot two. That's the right height. But she was five-six, and full in the body. After all her worry about what she'd do in retirement, she just died of a heart attack aged fifty-one. Then I knew I was on my own.

About my father. She didn't like discussing him. He must have been a shit, because he left her before I was born. I only met him once, when I was eighteen. That Easter his circus was at Crystal Palace, while ours was on Clapham Common. My mother said, You can go if you like, but she wouldn't go herself. So I sit at the back of the ring, waiting for him to come on with the horses. Why I sit at the back I can't think. He'd never seen me before. And when he comes on, all I can think is he's small, so *small*. I'd always thought of him as big. And he didn't look the least like me. (But then I don't think I look like anybody else.)

It was betraying Mama, but I wanted to like him. So I think, What the hell, and after the show I ask to see the horses. He takes me round the stalls tent, and all the time I'm thinking, How could Mama have chosen *him*? He was peaky and shifty-looking. He introduces me to a fat, hard-looking woman. This is my wife, he says, Bertha, the young lady has come to see the horses. (Fancy being called Bertha, you'd feel like a sunk ship.) Oh she says, and goes away.

As he was showing me the Shetlands, he slid an arm round me and pinched my bottom. I went cold inside. Then I slapped him. Not a light slap, but with all my shoulder and back and heart, like I'd kill him. I fancied Mama could hear the slap in Clapham.

I never told her I'd even spoken to him.

After Mama died, I couldn't leave the Applebys for another circus. I had to carry on her act. I used to hear her voice all the time, Grip harder, Straighten your pelvis, Don't look down. She often called out that – Don't look down. So all that time she must have been afraid of heights, and never told me.

In those days our circus was run like a circus should be. It was only when Appleby took over from his brother that trouble began. We had a whole lot of bad bookings right away. And that woman! You had to laugh. Suddenly every other spot included little dogs somersaulting and shitting all over the ring. Sometimes she fell over them. Then her turban would roll off and her ringlets shake free like a lot of shampooed puppies' tails, you could nearly hear them squeak. She wanted me to do an aerial act with a pug, but I said I'd drop it.

I feel sad for Appleby. He's quite out of his depth. But he's always been affectionate with me, kind of a father. So long as they let me go on developing, and we don't all stagnate, I'll stay.

But Mark! The moment I saw him I felt, here's somebody I can really get on with. All that life and inquisitiveness. I love that. He makes me think – and that's good for me.

It's wonderful and peculiar. I'm not certain what he sees in me. I feel uninteresting compared to him. I haven't had much time for thinking. I'd half forgotten about men, when he came to my wagon with all his questions. *Why? How? What?* I can't answer half of them. Mark always believes there's *more* to everything – and perhaps there is, but I don't know about it. I feel rather simple.

He's a beautiful lover, very gentle. Sometimes he takes me in my costume – he says he's sharing my act and my mystery. I don't know what my mystery is, but I feel I'm nearest myself in my costume. Then I'm really me.

He talks in his sleep. I can never make out a word. But later he always wants to know about it, and says you should write down your dreams the moment you wake. But mine make no sense, darling.

Our circus is pretty tatty compared to most, but I still love it. Mark doesn't, though. He finds it all a bit vulgar, what he calls flashy. He likes to think I'm superior to it, but of course I'm not. The other evening one of the girls came on in a catsuit lined with magenta feathers, and he kept saying, It's too much, *you'd never.*

I didn't admit her costume was one of my cast-offs.

I know he doesn't really belong with us. He wants roots. He ought to have a family. But when I saw her photograph on his locker, I wanted to smash it. She looked so natural there, just like a part of him. She makes church windows. I'm not the jealous type, I don't want her to be hurt – but I'm not coming second to anybody. It's just not my nature. I suppose I'm proud.

It's the same in the ring. The old spots bore me as soon as I've perfected them. I have to go on, higher and more difficult. I don't know what I'll do when I get old. Other trapeze artists spoil their acts. They use fancy props and get away with cheap effects. One girl I know has taken to showing the donkeys. Another dangles from trapeze wires posing in a half-moon, and doesn't do a thing. I'd rather kill myself than that. Perhaps Mama was lucky. I guess I'm like my friend Lizzie. She blacked out on a neck-spin and was just left dangling for a full minute. The she came down and took her bow. She didn't even realise she'd been out.

Mark asks me why I'm taking my handstand to the top. *Why? Why?* Typical Mark. And of course I don't know. But it's partly about control, and the body. You test yourself again. You have to. And then you master yourself. I can't explain.

Even when the circus is full of people, the handstand and angel-pose act make me forget them. The whole thing might last just ten minutes, but all your day has worked up to that. I go into the ring, and the clapping and music don't mean much. I just look up into the tent roof and think, Here goes . . . Then I leave everything behind me on the ground − crowd, friends, Mark. If it's a new venue I feel nervous, and it's good. Some trapeze artists don't like heights, but I love them. The higher I go, the better. On a windy day the canvas shakes. In summer you are climbing into a furnace. That can threaten your balance, and you have to watch. But the amber spotlight follows you up. It's wonderful. I've never been afraid to look down. I simply forget to. In any case, the spectators are in darkness. All you see below is a white pool of light and the front row of the ring. I don't feel I'm any height in particular. I'm just far up, alone. The music may be crashing out but I never hear it. There isn't any noise at all. There's hardly anything. Just me and this thin platform, with the forearm-brace. When I slide my arm into it and go into the balance, people say I look so frail, they're frightened. But it's most like swimming. That's why I don't like wearing the lunge. It attaches you. It's cheating. Wearing that, you're not really alone.

But instead, I go up the last nine feet. Then the roof is so close above, I see my shadow on its canvas, fading and growing. So I keep my eyes on the platform, and at the fourth wide swing, or the fifth, I go into the angel-pose. And that's the strangest feeling − the height, the swaying and my stillness all together. The emptiness everywhere around. That's what does it. I think it's the emptiness. And myself in it. Swaying. But controlled and motionless. Myself.

The other day Mark wanted to know what my greatest ambition was, and I've been thinking about that. It is this, darling. I'd like to have my own troupe. I'd be the star (that's only human), and at the climax I'd leave the trapeze bar for a triple somersault. But I wouldn't want anyone to catch me. I'd just want it to go on forever. Because that moment's not a preparation for any other moment. It's an end in itself. It's the real thing.

10

The long-term prisoners grow afraid they're going to die inside, and sometimes, lying on my bunk, I stare up at the cell ceiling where it arches to meet the wall, and share that fear. I become afraid my faculties are fading. The silence beyond the walls is less silence than throttled noise. I imagine my ears have failed. And the only way to test my long-distance vision is to climb onto the chair and look at the perimeter wall. I close my right eye to check if the left one is focusing, then close my left one; then I imagine the right eye sees better, or else is dimming. Even our range of smells is reduced – urine, disinfectant and an unidentifiable mustiness.

But on Thursday morning, after weeks of cloud, something new happened. The sun's trajectory has carried it across our window. Its light pierces our unchanging air. If I stand with my back against the door, I see its circle balanced in the window's square. Then it pushes a gold rectangle over the floor. The embrasure is so deep that the rectangle moves fast. It wrinkles across the concrete and ascends the mass of vulva and clitoris which is our wallpaper. They have long ago become sexless abstracts. But now they smirk into brilliant life. Then the light skews and vanishes.

After we are unlocked for the tea-queue, I jink into the next-door cell to share this prodigy. We're not supposed to visit cells without permission, but the screws turn a blind eye. They don't crack down on dope either – it keeps things quiet – and now I find Drinkwater high in a paradise of his own. But Brown only says: 'Sun? It didn't come in

82

here,' and goes on sticking up his collages. His face has acquired an unhealthy, lemon tinge. I wonder if he is ill. He has found the group photograph of a mililtary academy, and is inserting outsize babies among the cadets. The adjutant's head has become a clock.

I say: 'What's all that about?'

'Seems right.'

'That guy's head. Is that okay?'

'Yup.' His face is an elderly child's. It yields nothing.

'You're always asking questions.'

'Sorry.' I thought I'd given that up.

I go out and make my way to the chaplain's room instead of the tea-queue. I don't know why I've asked to see him again. I suppose his ginger cat's face is the most wholesome here.

He welcomes me with professional warmth. Behind his desk hangs the Christian paradox: the crucified god, enscrolled 'I am the resurrection and the life'. For a while we talk about this shadowy resurrection, while I sniff around the edges of his orthodoxy, faintly hoping for something. My voice sounds strained and pathetic to me. I deepen it. I float theories about transmigration and the relativity of Time, where lives are stamped for ever. I sound haywire. The priest, in any case, does not need these fantasies: he is safe with the authorised version. He does not address himself to my theories, but to my tone of voice, which trembles. Something has unfrozen in me. If he were not here, I would be weeping. I don't understand this. After so long, dry-eyed.

He says, to comfort me: 'You don't feel perhaps she *wanted* to die, do you? All her life, I mean. From what I understand, she seems to have taken unusual risks.'

'No.'

'But it is rather an unusual profession for a girl to choose, isn't it? The trapeze.'

'She didn't choose it. She was born into it. The circus is like that.' I hear my voice steadied. 'She loved it.'

83

I've just read an essay on suicide, and I badly want to quote it at him. But I cannot remember its words, and only find them now: *No evidence suggests that 'playing with death' is connected to a death-wish. On the contrary, surveys of racing-drivers, bullfighters and others indicate that 'courting' death is an act of heightened vitality. The subject rarely entertains any serious expectation of dying.*

But I cannot cite this at the time. I only say: 'I think people have a right to their own end.'

The priest looks sad, suddenly tired. I suppose he has heard this platitude often. He says: 'You don't think nature should take its course?'

'We interfere with nature's course all the time.' He has done me a service by irritating me. 'It seems the nature of everything to interfere with everything else.'

He hears the revived sharpness in my tone, and answers it with his own. 'It doesn't trouble you that suicide is wrong in the eyes both of the Law and the Church?'

'The Law and the Church never gave a damn about her.'

He shows a faint hint of anger, or the effort to control it. 'I take it you simply mean she didn't believe in God? If she had, she might be alive now.' He sits up pontifically. 'The Law and the Church agree that the disposal of life rests with God.'

Suddenly I'm furious. The man is just a mouthpiece. He looks like that too, all smiling lateral orifices. I'm half shouting: 'That law's just ecclesiastical gibberish! It's the same law that made attempted suicide punishable by death!' The mouthpiece has fallen silent, so I go on: 'I think a God who lets people linger with cancer or cripples them forfeits any right to guide their life. Anyway, she didn't believe. Why should she live by somebody else's god?'

The priest, I can tell, has sickened of this argument. He just wants to do a fade, as Morgan would say. But he composes himself, running his hands over his hair, and says: 'All the same, He's there.'

He manages to invest the words with stern conviction, as if calming a child. I must be in quite a state, I think. My hands are shaking so badly I stuff them in my pockets. My anger has drained away. I realise, too, how much I want to believe him. The strength of another is hypnotic when you are weak. Suddenly I'm saying: 'I'm sorry, Father [I'm calling him Father again]. You must wonder why I came to you.'

So do I. But I suppose I'd rather she was bored in his heaven or burnt in his hell than simply not exist at all. I stand up.

He says: 'Shall we pray together?'

I hover in front of his desk. 'No, I won't do that.' She would have despised that.

I go back, as slowly as I dare, to my cell. It's lock-up time, and the galleries echo with the emptiness I never normally see. The place has reverted to meshed daylight and steel: an aviary for men. A few screws are patrolling the catwalks. They look like zoo-keepers. They nod as I pass. Most of them are thick, simple men, who probably failed the police exams. They have their own stress. We quickly sum them up as bastards or soft touches. Some, like the fellow whose hair is falling out, can scarcely cope. Others are routinely oppressive, out of insecurity, I think. Still others – like the medical officer, jaunty from treating men he thinks worthless – have been desensitised by years of routine.

But I no longer feel in punishment here, or any surface humiliation. The landmarks I pass are just decorations in limbo: the wing post-box, the AIDS warning, the black-board notice, today scrawled: 'Whoever sent a letter to 44 Anna Street, Manchester, tell the censor who you are.' Some hope. For days I go without feeling anything much at all, except a distant fear of either staying or leaving. And even this numbness is not very distressing. Often I imagine myself substanceless, transparent. I matter hardly at all.

Then this blinding grief upsurges. As now, looking down

the well between the tiered landings, I see the iron meshes of our safety netting, preserving us.

Morgan grimaces as they let me in. 'You getting the glory, or what?'

'Just a way of seeing around,' I say.

The judas-hole in our door snaps open. Morgan goes quiet. It closes. He says: 'Lorrimer's been owing me for five weeks now. Says he's got four ounces of baccy. But I been up on the fours too much. Screws getting suspicious. How about you going?'

But I'm not keen to be his debt-collector. 'It can wait.'

'I don't think so, no.' His one good eye pleads cannily. 'Lorrimer could be going to Category A any time. And he's a wild card. Might do anything.'

'I've just been on the fours,' I say. 'Looks odd if I go back.'

Morgan's mouth shudders with a reply he can't get out. He shakes his head, to clear it. You might think his drugs racket was threatened with collapse (but he has eight more stuffed radio batteries). 'In ten minutes we'll be slopping out, and that's the time. Just ask the duty officer. It's Jackson today, he's a soft-cop. Say you're lending a book.' His voice is quavering. Perhaps he is remembering his past insolvency outside: the start of the downward slope.

I allow him to persuade me. Ten minutes later I'm outside Lorrimer's cell on the fours. They've been slopping out too, but have come back. The cell howls with pop music. On its walls, above the pin-ups, are urban landscapes clipped from some magazine. They hang there like windows on a grimmer world than Morgan's. It's an irony I can't digest. Morgan has painted a dreamscape of the outside, yet remains here almost content; whereas Lorrimer envisages harshness, and wants to go. He is standing sullenly above the table where a set of chessmen, loaned from wing office, deploys on a worn board. They are so abraded by fingering that the castles have become bishops, and the bishops pawns.

He lobs me a cigarette. 'What's doing?'

'Morgan wants his baccy. He thinks you'll do a fade and leave him broke.'

Lorrimer sniffs thoughtfully, then he rummages under his mattress and tosses me a tin. 'Tell him I won't be buying again. Got my own sources.'

'I'll tell him.'

'Hang on a moment.' He strides behind me, lifts the top from his locker and wedges it against the door. Then he turns up the already-screaming transistor. 'That's why they ban VHF in here. It'd knock a hole in the walls.' He laughs at my grimace. (In fact VHF is banned to prevent prisoners tuning in on the screws' network.) 'You got a wheeze for knocking holes in walls, Swabey?'

'Nope.' I wait for whatever he's after. In the nearby bunk the shriven face of Scotty turns to watch.

Lorrimer says: 'Keep your back to the judas.' Then he opens his fist against my chest. It contains a grooved roller, welded together from the metal bases of light bulbs – although where he found them I can't tell. The lights are all caged here. 'You knew circus trapeze gear, didn't you? You think this any good as a runner?'

I twist it in both my fists, and it holds. 'Can't tell. I never saw rollers used as trapeze equipment.' What the hell was he planning? The roller was threaded by a jagged hole. 'You'll need to smooth that out.'

'No problem. What sort of pins d'you use?'

'Look, Lorrimer, I don't know what the scheme is, but if you're planning to make it out on this thing, you've lost your mind. I've only seen rollers like this on block and tackle, and they're properly framed, with steel pins.' I thrust it back at him. 'Even if you make it, what are your chances of staying out there? Twenty to one? Thirty?'

'Don't sermonise me.' His fingers close over the roller. 'When are you getting out? October, isn't it? That's great. By then *I'll* be transferred to Maximum Security. For *twenty fucking years*. Getting out of here's a picnic compared to that.'

'You won't get out of here. Not with that thing.' I imagine him launching from his cell window on some crazy rope-act, pitching down into the dark. 'If you stay quiet, you'll be out before you're forty-five. That's not the end . . . You can start a life at forty-five. Get married, have kids. Lots of guys have a failed first career. Then they start again . . .' Yet all the time, even as the pacifistic sentences are passing my lips, I'm thinking: *Go. Get out. Make it.* 'Forty-five's the prime of life for some guys . . .'

Lorrimer's fist lands on my chest. 'Save your breath.' His whisper pierces clean through the music. 'I'd be finished by then, Swabey. I'd end up in the bat-house. Or I'd be a shell like Morgan – all that crap about stately homes and making it. I'd rather top myself. I'm not ending in the trash can like that . . .'

The skin has tensed back from his eyes and teeth, and I suddenly realise how deep in him runs this fear of inner decay, of the moment when something gives way, of the leaking-in of compromise, consoling fantasy. Because I know this in myself. Prison holds you up for breaking. Sometimes I listen to myself, listen for how much energy is left. And I can't gauge.

Lorrimer's stare is flailing me. 'Just you tell me, Swabey, tell me honest. If you were me, would you accept to moulder in the nick for twenty years? What would you do? *What would you do?*'

I hear myself say: 'I'd get out.'

The admission is a kind of trust. He recognises it. His fist opens on the roller again. 'Then tell me about this fucker. Is it strong enough to take my weight?'

'It may be. But it's too shallow, and probably too wide. Depends on the width of your rope.'

'It's not a rope. It's a one-inch cable.'

'Then you can afford to close the roller up and deepen it.' I wonder where on earth he keeps this cable. 'But it's the pin that'll take the strain. God knows what you can use. Bit of rawhide might be simplest.'

Our music is so loud that the screw is almost at the door before Lorrimer hears him and unwedges it. 'Lock-up!' the man bawls. 'Turn that thing down.' He is one of the loutish ones, sarcastic. He looks at me. 'What're you doing here?'

'I got permission from Jackson. I'm lending Lorrimer a book.'

The screw turns caustically to Lorrimer. 'Taken to reading, have we?' He fingers the book, a historical biography. His eyes narrow in theatrical distrust. 'You must be getting desperate.'

Lorrimer says mildly: 'Oh, I am.' And I make my way back to my cell.

11

I tried to deflect her from coming. I cited the long coach journey, and assured her I'd be out by the autumn. I anticipated her dismay, and hated the sheer incongruity of my mother entering a prison.

Yet as often before, she proves stronger than I expected. Through the lobby I glimpse her buying coffee from the WRVS woman, purposely delaying, perhaps awaiting her composure. She is dressed with awkward respectability, and has even put on a hat. Then she shuffles over, smiling, sits down and takes my hands fraily across the table. She doesn't think much of the facilities, she says. She wonders what our canteen is like – she scrutinises me for malnutrition – and what about washing? 'I suppose you wouldn't have your own bath . . .'

I don't tell her what the shower-room looks like. But there's a clinic, I say, a library, a gym and an exercise area – it begins to sound like holiday camp – and even a chaplain.

'Well, that's a comfort.' She fumbles in her carrier-bag to find the food she's brought me. 'You were always so religious as a boy. I wonder where all that went to.' She makes it sound like spots. 'Funny you mentioning the chaplain . . .'

Obliquely she is asking: 'Have you gone religious?' In our family important questions or demands were never broached outright. Instead we negotiated a labyrinth of byways and covered approaches, heralding our needs with time-honoured hints and allusions. So now I only say: 'The chaplain's nothing much.'

90

'Good.' She sips her coffee, not looking at me. 'It wouldn't be the right way to come to it.' She has this disconcerting way of saying something tough out of the blue.

I start: 'That's how they get you . . .'

But I am careful talking to her about religion. Near the end of her life, her claim on it seems delicate and necessary. It is seven months since I have seen her, and her hair looks ash-white under the striplight. She seems to have entered old age without my noticing when. I squeeze her hand. Her shoulders are heaving and falling with the effort of her breathing. She has been carrying the bag of food for me. She shows no self-consciousness or humiliation at being here. So once again she surprises me, and shames me for underestimating her.

She says: 'Who else has been visiting you?' The old querulousness is back in her voice. 'One visit every four weeks seems so little. They ought to change that.'

'Well, last month an old friend from the *Hampshire Times* arrived. The month before a fellow from the circus rolled up, and before that it was Katherine. She's coming again soon.'

'Katherine.' Mother's voice softens over the name. 'She's kept me in touch with how you are. Your letters sound quite all right, but you never know.'

'My letters are censored, I'm afraid.'

'Censored? Katherine didn't tell me that.' She looks perplexed. 'But she's a wonderful girl, a great looker-after, Marcus' — my childhood nickname always precedes cajoling. She stops suddenly, leans forward, other words wheezing in her mouth, then dying out. 'Just wait until I catch my breath.'

'Have you been taking your pills?'

'Oh yes.' She straightens with a little sigh. Isolated across the table, she appears even smaller than she is. All through my childhood, and after, she ruled us with her illnesses, routinely referring to herself as 'your poor sick mother'.

After my father's death I grew less tolerant of her. She had capitalised so richly in advance on her own death (all those sentences which started 'When I'm gone . . .'). But his had come suddenly. He'd had no time even to mention it.

Yet now that she is genuinely reaching the end, she no longer talks of it at all. Looking at her, I feel prematurely bereft. Under her raincoat, I know, her chest is barrelling out with emphysema.

She says softly: 'Where was I? Oh yes, Katherine . . . a wonderful looker-after. Better than I have ever managed.'

In family code, this means: I want to see you married before I die.

I say: 'Yes, she's at her best in crises. She understands everything.' But I am thinking how weak my mother has become. The skin of her neck shows silvery, like tissue. I am afraid she might be gone before my release. This is a chronic fear with prisoners, I know. But suddenly I feel I understand so little of her. Her youth is unimaginable to me. She never talks of it: the daughter of a piano-teacher from Exeter. And if I questioned her, I know, she would only frown nonplussed, and reassert the plaintive credo that her life has been mewed up, eventless. She seems to have been dying, piecemeal, all my life. 'I'll come and see you the day I'm released.'

'Yes do, do come.' She looks pleased. 'You'll be on your feet again in no time. You always did jump up after you'd been knocked down.'

'Did I?' My boyhood seems light years away.

'Yes, always. That's your father in you.'

I have become a mystery to myself. I smile at her. I have the sensation that when she leaves she will be taking most of me away with her, everything certain. I have lost any grip on my past. Clara's death, and prison, separate me from it. I seem to have crossed over some inner divide, leaving behind my mother, Katherine, half of myself. I can't grasp this. I only imagine it is irretrievable. It is as if Clara had drawn me to this far side, then disappeared.

* * *

Two nights ago I dreamed that a cable stretched between our prison wall and freedom. A figure was swinging across it in the night, but slowly, in difficulty. He looked slighter than Lorrimer, and was perhaps me. Soon he stopped moving altogether, and a spotlight picked him up in the dark. Then he fell.

I have this absurd fear now that my mother is going away, taking the heart of me, the explanation, with her. I say: 'Was I very restless as a boy? Destructive?'

'Destructive? No.' She looks faintly shocked.

'Self-destructive, I mean? Did I always go after the impossible?'

She pats the hair around her hat, delaying. She is not used to this. 'You were always a dreamer,' she says, 'if that's what you mean. Never quite content with anything. At night you used to fly in your dreams, you said. You were horrified when your old mother said she didn't. For you it was the main reason for going to sleep.'

Perhaps it is the patting of her hair, preliminary to leaving, or the stirring of the screws behind their desk, but my panic increases that she is carrying some solution away. 'But did I always want things, love things, out of my reach?'

Her face refocuses me. It quivers a little. Then she says with that sudden, confusing sharpness of hers: 'Was she out of your reach?'

But I am staring into my lap, unable to answer; and after a while she pushes her bag of food across the table. 'That's your supplement, dear.' Her expression has returned to its old plangency. She is hunting in her mind for advice, and finding nothing. One of the warders comes over to say that our time is up, and she labours to her feet. Her cheeks are dry and soft to my kiss, as she whispers goodbye. Sometimes I feel I have never known her at all.

12

Mark thinks I don't know, but he's like an open book, with his quizzical way of looking at me, and his lame excuses for being away so much, and his tender, guilty love-making. Is he thinking of her when he touches me? That would be unbearable. When I imagine that, I can't endure him to touch me at all. Then I close my eyes and mind together, and tell myself this circus-girl will pass, she must pass, and that one day we will talk about it, and he will love me for not complaining.

He's become more restless than ever; but while before I thought that is just Mark, that is his work, now I know I have grown boring. I knew this would come one day, I knew it, but not so soon. I can't hold him now at all. When he arrives here he often says he has work to do, and sits apart, or reads. I watch myself dimming in his eyes. He's not seeing me any more, but something inside his own head. I don't think I exist, I've just reverted to ugliness. I wonder all the time how I should behave, what will attract him. It's like playing to an audience which has gone. I always did this too much anyway, finding myself in his eyes, his mind, seeking approval. I seem to have learnt nothing at all, unless that to love is not always to be lovable.

So I've lost myself. I know the only way I should behave, keep my dignity, my attraction, is to be independent. Mark was always saying: Find yourself, Be yourself. But I don't know who this is. Perhaps in the end there is no way I can be, nothing I can do, just wait. I almost dread his coming now, which is terrible. I make feeble moves at independence. While he was reading in my studio the other evening, I decided there was a film I wanted to see, and that I'd go. Mark just said okay, didn't even look up; and halfway through the film I realised that I didn't understand a thing, that the screen was blurring with my tears, that I hadn't wanted to see it anyway. I'd just wanted him to say 'Don't go' or 'I'll come too.' ·

I try to be less demanding, but it doesn't work. I know all my petty sacrifices and disclaimers betray this pent-up want. I've become an insecure child. I would rather he was angry than just ignored me. The indignity of it is that for over a year I've been thinking I love him, I love him, and now I'm left with this thing 'love', which isn't a gift, unselfish, any more, but is just my need. So I go on screaming it inside me, even though he doesn't want it, and it's only my own hurt, and the memory of that lost abstraction which we called 'our love', and which I thought was indivisible, and might even last . . . I can't go on.

I realised, I think, on the summer evening we went to the theatre, but I smothered it away inside me, like one of those tiny fairytale demons which are incarcerated in barrels, then swell to shatter the kingdom. We saw a repertory company in Ibsen's *Peer Gynt*. In this rather beautiful story, the hero abandons Solveig, his childhood beloved, for a long quest through the world outside, and at last, almost broken, returns to her. This play turned Mark sombre, I noticed. He called me his Solveig teasingly, blusteringly, all evening, and I wondered whereabouts on his journey he conceived himself to be. Hadn't he yet come home?

We sat in a restaurant with candles, bad food and musical wallpaper. Mark likes these places, thinks they're romantic, while I'm irked by the waste of them and would like to be cooking something better, more leisurely, at home. But I was happy to sit in his gaze, of course, and talk about the play, and what we'd been doing.

Casually, it seemed, he mentioned her, a trapeze girl called Clara, but the way he spoke her name – a cadence on its first syllable – woke a distant alarm. I think since then I've never been at ease. He talked about the circus and gypsies and rootlessness, while I wondered who is this Clara, then hid the question away.

'Wouldn't it be marvellous,' he said, 'to find some society utterly different from your own, and immerse yourself in it?' He's always wanted to travel. 'Togo, say, or Burma?'

'I'd be frightened.'

He was picking at the cataract of dead candle-grease. 'Don't you ever feel a need just to take off somewhere? *Anywhere*, almost?'

'Where would we go?'

He began shredding the candle savagely. 'I think it would be good to lose your own certainties for a year or two, don't you? Disappear into somebody else's culture?'

But I didn't think so at all; I didn't even think it possible. 'Only if I liked the culture,' I said.

'That's the point. It ought to be one you *didn't* really like.'

'Then I probably wouldn't condone it.'

His fingers tore at the spent tallow. He looked angry. Its grease spattered the table-cloth.

I said: 'Watch out.'

Then, premeditatedly, he flicked the pool under the wick with his finger, so the drops fell on my plate. It was a tiny act, but it was the first time he had ever done anything against me. That sounds overwrought, I know – just the spatter of red candle-grease on china – but I felt it with a rush of sadness and alarm, as if some door had opened in him, some door I'd never known, and that he would even be capable of hating me.

Several times after this, as he arrived for weekends, he

96

called me Solveig in a jocular tone tinged with self-reproach, and I took this to be a signal between us, as if he were saying Wait, wait, and I was touched with hope.

Not long ago, when we had supper in his flat, I picked up the anthology he was reading. It fell open at a poem about love in unfaithfulness, as if he had left it there for me to find. I had to turn away from him and pretend to be reading it by the light of a farther lamp.

Later, in my own home, I gave way to this storm inside, alone, and let it blow itself out where no one could hear. I felt I would never see again. But in the mirror, at dawn, my eyes were just swollen frog's eyes, and I managed to laugh at them, and it's another day.

I had to see her, she had eaten into me so. I had to see what I had not become for him. In my mind she had grown into a creature of supernatural distinction. A circus girl, yes, that was strange, but she must be a unique one, who brought some special poetry to what she did, someone who deserved that cadence on her name. I don't know whether I wanted to hate or admire her.

I located the circus half a day's journey from Peterhurst, squatted on a village green. I half expected to find his car parked there, but it wasn't, and there were hardly any. I don't know what I had expected, but not this, it was so small and damp and wretched. A dreadful band struck up in a curtained gallery, then the ring was full of men and girls in scintillating coats and bikinis, doing cartwheels and balancing on ponies. How have these shows survived, they're so debased, an insult even to children?

When they announced her entrance, I couldn't even guess what was coming. Then the curtains parted and in pranced this vulgar girl in a grotesque conjuror's cape and feathered coronet. Her eyes were ludicrously made up, and she wore fishnet tights. I felt a physical sickness, not because of her – she was just an ordinary trapeze girl – but because this glittering absurdity was Mark's beloved. It seemed as if there had entered into the ring some dark taste in him, some region I didn't know. As she climbed her pole half naked, I thought of his hands on her – she had a good figure – and his mouth on that crease of crimson lips. Why I didn't leave then I don't know, I just sat paralysed in my seat, thinking how could he. People were even clapping.

She must have been either brave or insensitive, because I saw no safety-net. I've never understood athletics – so much energy creating nothing – and this was closer to that than to dance. She executed a handstand at one height and posed at another, but it was an effort to connect Mark's *Hampshire Times* review with anything she did. Apart from her courage, I couldn't see why her act was meant to be so uplifting. After she descended she barely waited for applause, but tripped away through the curtains as if we weren't there at all, or she didn't care.

But the moment she'd left, I confess I felt confused. I knew I'd seen her only in jealousy. She had simply come and gone in ten minutes, dedicated to a feat I never understood, and perhaps she was handsome in her showy way, and perhaps adept at what she did, if you liked that sort of thing.

Afterwards I walked among the caravans of these strange people, wondering which was hers. It was starting to drizzle. A woman in cap and overalls came from the tent and asked me who I wanted, and I could only say Clara, I remembered no one else.

'That's me!' she said.

She was so small, and older than I'd thought. I just stared at her rudely, and murmured some lie about her act.

'I'm so glad you liked it.'

I could see now it was her, the slight figure, the gauntness and rouged cheeks.

'Do you want a coffee?' she said.

I told myself I hadn't planned this masque, but I knew I hadn't meant to leave without speaking to her. When I climbed into her sitting-room, it seemed haunted by Mark. Nothing of his was visible, but I imagined him inhabiting it, relaxing on the plastic chairs, brewing himself tea, embracing her. He might have deserted me for another planet. It had hideous ormolued lamps and printed curtains. There were colour photographs of trapeze acts in gilt frames. The only books were sagas and adventure stories; a cassette recorder had been playing *The Nutcracker Suite*; and a tart, cheap scent was in the air.

'D'you take sugar?' she said.

Even in this soft light, you could never call her pretty. She did have fine eyes, but her features were irregular and too thin. I couldn't tell what he liked or found in her. I never could gauge sex-appeal. I just sat there dazed.

While she made the coffee, I went on pretending to be a fan, and loathed myself. 'Aren't you frightened up there?' I said.

'A bit. But that's part of the excitement.'

'I think I'd just freeze.'

'I froze once in rehearsal,' she said, 'the first time I ever went up. But my mother ordered me down, and calmed me, and it never happened again. Do you want milk? A little fear is good, I think.'

She might have been a Martian. 'Is that why you do it?'

She laughed. 'You sound like my boyfriend. He's always saying "Why?"'

I felt I might weep, or be sick. She said: 'But up there you don't ask yourself. You have too much else to think about – your physical control, not losing concentration, and all that.'

She was so composed, confident in the bright patina of her talk, yet underneath, I sensed, a little cold. Selfishly I thought: they won't get married, he couldn't marry her.

But as she handed me the coffee and sat down, she started to stare at me with the strangest pain. Perhaps it was my accent which made her suspicious, I don't know.

But she was gazing at my face as if she recognised me. She suddenly asked: 'What do you do?'

'I'm a secretary,' I said.

Then her face cleared, while I felt degraded that I'd been made to lie, because she was naïvely honest.

'You just reminded me of someone,' she said. But her voice trailed away and I didn't ask who, I was scarcely likely to know them. I could not imagine her circle of acquaintance anyway, even if she had one, or how someone lived like this perpetually on the move.

'How do you get hot water?' I asked.

'We all plug in to the electric generator when we arrive. Do you want to see?' She opened a door. 'This is the shower. And everything else works off propane gas.'

'That's very compact.' I peered in. It looked so makeshift and transient. 'Don't you ever want to settle down?'

'I'd hate it!' Her arm was stretched out against the door. She beamed at me. 'I'd feel everything was over!'

Suddenly a fleeting intensity irradiated her, something to do with her eyes, and for a bewildering moment I thought: Yes, she's rather beautiful. I even realised how Mark saw her. This eerie instant passed, but it left behind it a confused jealousy. Foolishly I felt that she might switch on this radiance at will, and had done so just to show me, but of course that's absurd.

As I left, she said: 'Look in again!'

She was so innocent, I felt diminished. I don't know what I'd hoped to achieve, but seeing her has only made confusion. I want to go back to despising her.

13

Katherine is still unused to this. The tension tears her face until she has settled opposite me, then her saddened calm comes seeping back, her mouth softens slightly, and her hands arrange themselves into their painterly stillness on the prison formica. The gaze of the other prisoners hovers over to her with the worship which handsome women elicit here. She is aware of them this time and shifts her chair so that she is shielded behind me.

After several minutes, sensing their gaze slacken, and not knowing what to talk about, she asks: 'What have most of them done?'

'A mass of things.' Our hands touch, without holding. 'This prison's a clearing-house.' Looking round, I realise how we all know about each other's case. It's odd. 'The fellow behind you's on remand for armed robbery, the chap on your left is a nonce, and – '

'A what?'

'A sex-offender.' I've picked up the language without noticing. 'I don't know what he did. They're kept separate.'

She doesn't look round; and sometimes, amongst all the other emotions sweeping her face, I catch confused glances of alienation, even of awe, that I am sitting here with these others – robbers, rapists, murderers – as if she cannot conclusively separate me from them.

'Two tables behind me you'll see my cell-mate Morgan.' I add jokingly: 'He's probably receiving hash right now.'

She tilts her head to glimpse him. 'What, that old man? He looks so *old*.'

'He's in his late-sixties. He's a con-man. He noticed you last time you came. You're his pin-up.'

She tilts her head back again. 'Oh.'

In my memory I try to reconstitute her younger face. I don't trust myself, but I see it bloom almost unlined. Now, for all its proportion, it is subtly dulled and loosened. I find this hard to bear, although it is not precisely unnatural to her. It is more as if her old vulnerability of expression had spread and deepened.

Walking in September fields, the weight of our silence at last became unsupportable. All along the hedgerows the molehills were scattered like crouched rabbits. Her arm was linked in mine, her face averted. But I knew its expression. It was worn away by waiting. We went down to a stream crowded with beech and holly. The sun picked out the water's trembling, where it fanned out under rocks.

Katherine said: 'It's lovely.' She darted me one of her supplicating looks, as if its beauty, like hers, could not exist without my confirmation.

'Yes, it is.'

We followed a glade of leaning ash trees, some fallen. Our silence grew. Our boots rasped along banks glazed with leaves. There were mossy stones, rabbits' droppings. Her fingers were curled over my forearm. I said: 'I've been seeing someone else.'

'I know.' Her hand slipped from my arm, departing into her loneliness. She must have dreaded these moments a long time.

I said: 'It's got serious.' Each word irretrievable.

'Yes.' She was walking out of reach.

I said: 'You know who it is?' then felt ashamed for displacing onto her the pain of telling.

'Yes.'

So she had gone ahead of me, suffered it, on her own. But I had no idea how much she knew, or understood, or forgave. I watched her profiled face, but it betrayed no

102

specific insult, bitterness or incomprehension: only a speechless hurt of its own. My throat clamped down on any words of apology or sorrow. They had turned shallow before I could utter them. I said: 'Was it so obvious?'

But she only let out a shudder of air, rank with disdain. It relegated me to the herd of my whole crass sex, perpetually disadvantaged, insensitive, unable to understand.

I searched for any alleviation. 'You and she are quite different from one another.'

She said: 'You don't have to make excuses.' Her tone, at once virulent and dead, told me I had gone beyond excuse. Nothing I said would mean anything. However true, my words would only be sounds. Her face was clenched. She was unrecognisable. I felt I had denatured her. The stream's lisp and our boots' rustle burst on the quiet. She said nothing more. Her change seemed irreversible, almost chemical: the change I had made. It stood in heartrending contrast to her old gentleness and self-distrust.

Under the jail's striplight, I see the face reassembled, still palely attractive, back in its flawed peace. Some joke I've made leaves the smile on it, forgotten. I scrutinise her for my old self. I identify my protectiveness, my affection, and a sickness which can't be answered.

That day still jars as if I might have prevented it. But of course I couldn't. Clambering over fallen branches, shelving earth, it was I, for some reason, who kept asking questions: 'How long have you known?'

She seemed not to have heard, was staring at the ground. Then she said: 'Always. Right from the start. Even *before*.' She looked at me. 'I always felt you were on loan to me.'

The pathos of this made me want to touch her, but she shied off, her hands delved in her pockets, walking parallel with me but closer to the stream.

'You always felt I'd leave?'

'Yes.'

'Do I seem so alien then?'

Her words were those of love; but deformed by the hardness of her voice, they became accusation: 'No, you're like the missing part of me.' She added in bitter self-annihilation: 'You're all of me in a way, if you want to know.'

I couldn't find an answer. I said: 'I always felt I was coming home to you.'

'That doesn't sound very exciting. But I suppose exciting is what she gives you.'

'She's different. You don't compare.'

She asked with stark simplicity: 'Then how could you love us both?'

That was why, I felt: because she and Clara nowhere touched one another. But the split in me, the diversity of need, I didn't understand. I said: 'I don't know.' The question momentarily obliterated itself, because I couldn't love this changed Katherine. I only felt abhorrence at what I had done to her. 'You belong to different parts of me.' Whatever I said sounded selfish.

She stopped on the path, her back to the stream. She was flushed with contempt. 'And what part does that girl belong to?'

'You don't know her.' I could sense how fragile she was, but my own temper was rising. 'You've never met her. You think just because she's – '

'I have met her.' Her defiance was tinged with embarrassment. 'I went to see her trapeze act. I was trying to understand. She didn't know who I was. We talked in that caravan.'

I felt an odd sadness that she had done this. It seemed to deplete her. It was as if Clara owned both of us now. I said: 'And you think she's so much less than you?'

'She's nothing to do with me. It's what she is to you that matters, and it's easy to see what that is. I presume she's just a body.'

I knew my anger would blind me as I spoke. I also remembered the instant I had lost myself to Clara, as she stretched up on tiptoe, and above the turquoise bodice her back had trembled into life. But how could I ever explain it? That a body was not just a body. Like a wavelength, it might transmit to one person's needs, but starve another's. Clara's carried a lodestar's separateness. It was not that she kept any secret in her – she would have laughed at that. But just as Katherine's body had warmed, confined, so Clara's, by its self-sufficiency, elicited this fervent disquiet.

But in my blundered words this, to Katherine, seemed only an excuse for lust. She said: 'You're trying to dignify yourself, and her.'

'She doesn't need me to dignify her.'

'Well to me she seemed . . .' But she choked back. 'I just can't imagine what you talk about.'

I couldn't answer at once. It seemed to me that Clara and I just chatted about ordinary things, drank coffee together, and were happy. I said: 'Of course she's not cultivated. She's had no chance to be.'

But this defence seemed to infuriate Katherine, as if it were an attack on her own values. Her words came scathing, unrecognisable: 'Does she think at all? Can she write?'

'She's an acrobat. She just *is*!' I was half shouting. 'She's what people write *about*.'

'That silly review of yours!'

We seemed to lie in ruins. 'It was what I felt.'

'You're besotted by her glamour. I can't believe it. It's just tinsel. She's utterly ordinary.' Her words were pared to bone. 'You're in love with a circus turn. That's what she is.'

I was engulfed by tiredness. My feet seemed rooted in leaves. I said: 'It expresses her, that's all. As your glass expresses you.'

Katherine started walking again. 'I'd hoped mine would be enough for you.' She sounded spent.

My voice said: 'So had I.'

We reached the head of a gulley filled with half-toppled

trees. She went in front of me. Her head was tilted back a little. I caught up with her at a barbed-wire fence, which she seemed too tired to climb. The tears were pouring down her cheeks. When I touched her, her eyes wandered my face in a disconnected panic, as if looking for her identity there. Then she averted her face and said into the air: 'You did mean it, didn't you, Mark? You did feel it? Us, I mean.' Her voice broke. Her hands lifted to her face. 'You weren't just pretending to love me?' Even the past was being taken away from her.

She did not seem to hear my answer. But when I held her shoulders she buried her head against me. Her fingertips clung to my collar. At last she said softly, the words gutted of reproach: 'You seem so rootless sometimes. I'm not sure you really want to be loved.'

This disquieted me, reverberating like a half-truth. Holding her tensed yet separate against me, I felt as if I were repudiating a whole familiar and constricting world for something which floated unearthed. It was like stepping off the ground and into air. I even received a faint, chill intimation that it was not possible.

A little later Katherine's fingers loosened from my collar and she detached herself, her fists still clenched at her breast. Then she turned, sighing, and leant with her back against me, as if practising how to be alone. So we stared down the ruined aisles of beeches to the stream, which looked too puny to have carved this gulley of dying trees.

She said: 'I'm sorry I spoke like that about Clara. She's a brave girl. I just wasn't sure if she's . . . our sort of person.'

Our sort of person: the words echoed from somewhere I was leaving. They may have slipped out involuntarily. They invoked the loves and values which we had perhaps shared too snugly, too exclusively. Clara didn't listen to Schubert.

So I found myself transplanted, even before Clara's death, or these tentative times of healing, when we stare across the prison table and wonder what is left of us. Katherine, of course, is looking at me from the changed state to which I abandoned her, and she, I think, can no more return to me than I to her.

14

It had been raining all day. The circus glittered in the city's park – the neon-lit 'Appleby's Big Top' had been restored – and already a few families were parked under the trees. On Friday nights the 'proper local folks', as Appleby called them, were mixed with London commuters. The crowds grew but their enthusiasm lessened. Then the clowns and the conjuror, who were Lancashire men, and the mucker who had run away from school in Durham, would gossip nostalgically about the North, where crowds roared and cheered properly, they said, and spent real money.

I arrived an hour before the evening performance, and walked through slush towards the caravan-village. All week Clara had been beyond my reach, but the hours were studded with knowledge of her: now she'd be practising her perch act, now washing her hair (arms folded round her head in the cramped shower), now touching her toes behind the ring curtains. Every day a host of tiny coincidences would conspire to remind me of her, just as they do here, in this prison, where so little new happens, and so little relates to anything outside, that you would expect to be reminded of nothing at all.

I came suddenly on the Applebys. They were in their overalls, clearing a drainage canal from the stables tent. She was saying: 'I'm fed up with this. We'll get a proper mucking team if we merge.'

'We will if we merge, dear.' Then they straightened up, both at the same time, and saw me. Even she looked disconcerted.

'Just talk,' she said.

'Merging with who?' I asked.

'It's only at the talking stage. *Nante parlare.*' Appleby hid in circus slang, took my arm. 'It would only upset things if news got out. So we'd be grateful . . . and yes, things are only at the talking stage. Very vague still. Very.'

We wandered towards their wagon, they with their spades, I with my briefcase. She said: 'We don't want to alarm the others.' They asked me in for a drink. They must feel badly in my power, I thought.

The wagon was infested with miniature dogs – pekes, pugs, poodles – which yapped at me from cushion-lined shelves and cupboards all round the room but scarcely moved. 'It were best you don't tell Clara,' Mrs Appleby said. 'It might just upset her, and you wouldn't want that, would you? Even if we did merge, nobody's going to lose their job. And if they do, it won't be our Clara, will it dear?'

'Certainly not,' Appleby said.

I could not tell if the prospect pleased or dejected them, because I think they did not know themselves. To merge with another circus would dilute their identity but increase their security: a common bargain. I said: 'What trapeze artists does this other circus have?'

'I think it's best not talked about,' said Mrs Appleby.

Then I realised that in my heart, cruelly, I wanted their circus to fail. I wanted to ground Clara in my life. But I knew also that this way she would be drastically reduced to us both, and that some better arena had to be found for her.

Now Appleby was preparing for the ring, smoothing the hair up from his ears over the tell-tale fringe of his toupee, and brushing his top-hat with his sleeve.

I said: 'Have you ever thought of retiring?'

'Oh no.' His voice went breathy with reproof. 'Who'd manage the circus if we did that?'

'Nobody,' answered Mrs Appleby. Her eyes jabbed round

the tiers of dogs. 'And what would *you* do? No, my dears, retirement wouldn't suit *you* at all . . .'

I finished my lukewarm beer and mumbled thanks. 'How's Clara's act?' She had been performing her heightened handstand for only two weeks, and was already starting to invest it with her peculiar intensity.

Appleby said: 'Solid as a rock.'

I made my way over the sodden grass. A thin drizzle had started up, and was blowing in folds across the lights above the tent. The Alsatians grumbled under canvas. I had almost reached her wagon when Barry came shambling alongside, carrying a length of duckboard over his shoulder. I wondered if he had heard anything about a merger. I said: 'How's the perch-act going?'

'No problems.' He upended the duckboard in the slush and jerked his thumb at her door. 'She's getting to be a dab-hand with the juggling.'

'You think you'll develop that spot at all? What about the future?'

But his face remained a tundra. Its yellow locks haloed it in ignorance. 'Dunno. Clara and me, we just had this idea of a revolving star act. Maybe get it together next year. We get winched up to thirty feet, then she does a toe-hang.'

I could not envisage it. Barry lifted the board again, and trudged off. I groaned at the drizzle. In my imagination the whole circus went faltering on indefinitely, reinventing itself piecemeal, patching and padding and stringing out into the twenty-first century. I could not know that tonight would be the last time I would see it. I imagined Clara as the vivifying heart around which it revolved. It might decay about her, I thought, but she at its centre was invulnerable.

'You're early!' Her arms circled me, their fingers splayed back, wet with greasepaint. She lifted her face to me with her controlled elation, extending her cheeks to be kissed, because they were newly made up, then dabbed at the greasepaint scuffing my chin and mouth.

We dropped onto the sofa. She was wearing a spikey costume for her perch-act with Barry: a crimson tutu with a gold lamé waist. I slowly kissed off her lipstick as we exchanged news. She knew all about the merger. 'Oh yes, everybody knows.' She was bubbling with laughter. 'And now *you* know! How do *you* know when you've only just arrived?' She held my ears. 'Who've you been eavesdropping on?'

'Just those Applebys.' I grasped her shoulders. 'If they merge it will be a good opportunity for you to get out. You've done your bit by them. If you push yourself with one of the bigger managements, they'll take you. You won't even have to ask for much money, because I can keep us.'

'You couldn't keep me for ever,' she said, without noticing the words' melancholy. 'These wagons take some repairing. I refuse to be a drain on you.' She stood up, fluffing out the net layers of her skirt, and crossed to her dressing-table. 'Anyway, I don't think there's any real chance of a merger. That other circus just wants to buy our stock. We'd be finished as a troupe.'

She sat in the white-lit ambit of her dressing-table now, repainting her face. Her voice quietened. She was sliding away into her mirrored self-appraisal, mentally approaching the ring. I said: 'What trapeze artists do they have?'

'They've got a man-and-wife flying trapeze act. But they're not exciting any more.' She laughed. 'She's had four children. They've settled for playing safe.'

Her twinning of family with safety was typical, but she herself loved children. During the interval she often put on overalls to sell clown-masks to the families in the crowd. She looked so different then, so much smaller than in the ring, that they scarcely ever recognised her.

'You should have children.'

Her laugh came from farther away than before. 'Where would I *keep* them? They'd have to go on shelves like Mrs Appleby's dogs.'

111

I could only reply by laughing. But these minutes have grown vivid in my memory: cherished because they were the last. She stayed intent on the bird-like acrobat in her mirror. She touched up the white and gentian round her eyes, slanting her head. I watched them in the glass, enormous and glittering, and the gentle cleft between her breasts. She said something about needing more moisturiser in winter. We could hear the band playing over the green. Once she asked in her cooled voice: 'Have you seen Katherine? I hope she's getting better.' She spoke as if Katherine must perfectly recover. She did not understand. Clara would never place herself in anyone's power, I thought, not even in mine.

I said: 'I telephoned her. She sounded . . . better.'

'Good.'

She lifted her hands to her hair. I remember how the costume looked coarse against her cream skin. Outside, the band was playing the conjuror's music now, a few minutes before her act. She rubbed some ointment into a fingernail, which had split from too much rosin. Then she said: 'Let's go,' and we went out into the drizzle.

Barry was already in the ringside tent, clasping the steel perch. 'Got a big crowd tonight,' he said.

Clara started jogging lightly, circling her arms. Then she arranged her cape in the looking-glass, confirmed the set of her shoulders, her neck, and smiled. She said: 'They've put those stinking paraffin-blowers on.'

Outside, modest applause went up, and the curtains opened to readmit the conjuror, carping at his assistant. Appleby's voice, amplified into confidence by the microphone, announced: 'And now ladies and gentlemen, a brand-new act . . . a round of applause please . . . will you welcome . . .'

They had gone through the draperies. Soon afterwards I heard the music mounting as she climbed the perch-ladder. Through the chink in the curtain my view was blocked by the mucker's back, and I went round to the front entrance.

She was balanced on the twenty-foot perch when I arrived, concentrating on the hoops which she cast and caught in the air. The band gushed, and the crowd responded. Finally, balanced on one leg, she revolved the hoops at her outstretched wrists and elbows. Her smile spread. I found myself smiling back. She was happy. I remember the living quality in her arms, white and supple. She looked like an aerial child, playing with golden toys.

When the interval came, I left her alone. She had to change her costume and focus on her new performance. A school-friend of mine was in the audience with his wife and child, and I sat beside them for the second half. The dogs' football spilled into the audience by mistake, bringing gusts of laughter; but under its yellow turban Mrs Appleby's face quivered with chagrin. The elephants ploughed through their drill. The clowns blustered. Then, hoarse from its day's announcements, Appleby's voice rasped out: 'And now, in a unique performance, ladies and gentlemen, taking her act to new heights . . .'

I remember thinking, as she climbed the pole, that the crowd was one of the largest we had drawn. Her act was still new enough to engage even our own people, and the ring curtains parted in the dark before a cluster of faces tilted back to watch her ascent. She climbed in a new costume: white and silver. It seemed to redefine her, to turn her more absolute, as if she were hardly earthly at all. The band was playing more crisply, I thought. Clara always said that up there she never heard them, yet she seemed to know instinctively when their drum-rolls and cymbal-clashes had come too late or early. Tonight, as she swayed her pole for the angel-pose, the cymbals sounded at the climax, and there was a trickle of spontaneous applause as she froze, her profile lifted clear beneath the silver cap, and her arms outstretched.

In the hush, as she ascended to the summit, I heard the patternless drumming of rain on the roof. I remember hoping it would not distract her. I wish now I could recall her every look and change. Above the swaying platform, brilliantly spotlit, she unbent with the same serene control, and hung there in a still, white curve through four or five arcs while the music faded.

Then, high up, sounded a tiny snap. I saw her right arm shifting loose in the forearm-brace. The metal had broken. If she had immediately unbent she could have seized the pole and saved herself. But to the last moment she tried to keep her poise, and appeared to drift away from the platform into the air. The spotlight, out of habit, followed her figure down. She fell headlong. I covered my eyes. But I heard her hit the ground.

15

Some get it like a fever. Then if they really want to escape they have to. You can't let it ride for ever. I reckon Lorrimer's like that, and thank Jesus he's not in our cell. Just me and Mark makes a tidy two, and we don't talk no bullshit about escapes.

This fucking peter is six paces long by three wide. Its floor is concrete solid down to twelve feet, and if you got through that, you'd find yourself in some other bloke's cell. Fat lot of use that. The window bars are thicker than a bloke's wrist. They check the bars and locks every day, and sometimes they do a spin on you out of the blue, no reason.

Yet all you hear in this nick is escape, escape, escape. Hurley reckons he's flitting out dressed as a visitor. Mitchell plans hiding in the skip outside the guv's office and getting carried out free, no charge. But funny how plans are never followed up. We'll do a runner, they say. But in the morning, there they are, grinning their mutton-brained heads off.

But I reckon Lorrimer's not like that. He's more the real stuff. He's in here for the big chill and doesn't mean to wait around. For sure he'll end up in Maximum.

These local nicks aren't so bad, and with Mark I'm onto a winner. I reckon there's more class in our peter than in the rest of this nick chucked together. We've got proper order in here. Things are tidy, and we know where the boundaries are. You only have to look in some of these other slams to see the difference. Just beasts in there, some of them, holes in their vests, feet on the table, fag-ash on the floor. But here we keep respect. I always did try to be nicely turned out. You got to keep respect.

I admit, when Mark first arrived I thought Christ, I'm being paired with a fucking screwball. He looked like he'd blanked out. He wouldn't hardly speak. Just sitting in his own skull. You can take this for a week or two, but not for months. When I tried to perk him up with stuff about getting out soon, he looked at me like I was mad. I don't think he thought the out even existed.

He's steadied now, though. Taken to reading and that, but gone off the Monopoly. He don't go blithering on about his sentence either, like Brown and the rest. In fact he wouldn't talk about the girl for months, not the one that was in the papers. He just dummied up. But nights he talks in his sleep, like he was haunted. Dreams and memories hit it big with us. They're our way to the out, and no one can stop them.

One night I hear him blubbing like he was a kid, fast asleep. Christ, I thought, I'm in the shithouse here, because he's not the blubbering type. Then he wakes up and goes and stares out the window, like he was firming things up in his head again. It's the only time he's ever talked about her, he was so done up. Says he was looking for her grave in his dream and found it. It was one of them cremation slabs, very small, he says. It just said 'Clara the Swallow'. Like it was a pet's grave.

He hasn't talked about it again, and I've kept mum. As I said, we know the boundaries. I just told him, Look, you do what you have to. I'd just heard this stuff on the radio, a professor bloke talking about life and why people turn out like they do. Things live out their basic natures, he says. You can't change their basic natures. They're just implanted. And I buy that.

I remember as a kid at school I was already conning. We used to fire off cardboard planes from elastic catapults. This elastic got to be our currency, like baccy is here, and I did a fast trade in it. There was a special expensive kind I got

116

from my dad's shop, and I'd flash a bit of this around like I had scads of it. I used to flog it for five packets of sherbet a strip, then ring in my show piece for cheaper stuff on the sly. Scooped the pool that way, and never got done. So I reckon it was implanted right from the start, because nobody ever taught me. It just came natural.

But when I ask Mark, he says he doesn't know his basic nature. At that age, he says, he was still an innocent. His folks sent him to innocent-type schools. So he was just living in a garden, as he puts it. He makes it sound like the Garden of Eden, so I ask where's the snake?

And he points at his heart and laughs.

16

People said Clara was lucky to be alive. For four days she remained in the intensive care unit of the local hospital, then she was transferred to a specialised centre for paraplegics. For two more days no one was allowed to see her. I took indefinite leave from work, and waited through the mornings in the hospital annexe with her circus friends. Then the circus moved on, and I was left alone.

Sometimes I felt unendurably light, as if there were some part of myself to which the truth had not penetrated. Then I would try to bore through this anaesthesia into the basement of real feeling by telling myself out loud what had happened. But it didn't work. I seemed to be as paralysed as she. Only once or twice I was hit by a ferocious guilt: that in my possessiveness I had willed her to the ground.

Wheelchairs were normal traffic along the hospital's ramps and corridors, but I could not connect her with one. In the wards I glimpsed young men mostly, dangled over their chairs or lying on beds. Others were watching small black-and-white television sets. A few took fragile steps with baby-walkers.

At last, at the week's end, the consultant called me in. He was an elderly, forthright man whose distanced sympathy must have been forged in countless interviews like this. I sat beside his desk in a room whose humdrum details I'll never forget. He said: 'Are you her only relative?'

'Her parents are dead. I'm her boyfriend.'

His hands rested lightly on a sheaf of X-rays and reports. 'I have to say that at this stage we are generally cautious

118

about giving a prognosis, because it's often hard to differentiate between shock and a real lesion. In shock the paralysis is only temporary, and feeling generally returns within six weeks. But in this case, I'm afraid' – the words 'I'm afraid' shook in isolation – 'the X-rays are virtually conclusive.'

He stood up and clipped one to the viewing-box behind him. Clara's neck appeared as a hazy ladder of wedge-shaped vertebrae. Only the faintest displacement of one wedge, and a slight darkening, showed at the tip of his pointing finger. It seemed such a little difference. He said: 'There's a fracture dislocation between the second and third cervical. Now I shall be frank with you' – the softening of his voice emptied my stomach – 'it indicates a badly transacted or severed spinal cord.' He switched off the box, sat down. His stare was assessing me for strength. God knows what it saw. 'Basically this means that all control or sensation below the neck has gone.'

I gazed back at him out of my trance. Even confirmed in his words, I did not believe it. I felt he could reverse the whole prognosis simply by saying something different. I waited. He said: 'Obviously this means that most of the body's ordinary functions are interrupted. In Cervical Two patients the interruption to the sweat glands means they can't control the body temperature as efficiently as you or I. So these patients are unfortunately often rather feverish or cold.'

I tried to catch up with his words while he sifted her reports. He went on: 'One of the major problems is pressure sores. You or I automatically shift position when we feel discomfort. But of course these patients don't experience pressure. To prevent the sores opening up and becoming gangrenous, we change her position every two to three hours. In the night, also. But it's done very simply, with an electrically moving bed.'

'I see.' But I did not. Everything he said sounded temporary to me. Such treatment could only apply to passing conditions, to severe but fugitive diseases. It could not be for ever. My voice had gone hoarse. But I tried the words: 'You mean she'll *never* . . . ?'

'Her face and neck, yes. But otherwise, no. Although some patients do experience slight vibrating and burning sensations.' He saw my face, and his voice forcibly brightened. 'She'll receive regular physiotherapy. We keep the muscles properly toned, to prevent contractures and blood clotting. We don't let them deteriorate.'

I seemed to have gone dead. I had nothing to say. But my voice asked: 'What can she *do*?'

'Well, she can watch TV, of course, and listen to the radio. And she'll be able to read when she can manage a page-turner. That can be done by head-movements nowadays. It's amazing, the devices that are being developed. There's a whole new system for tetraplegics. It works on breath – by suck and blow. They can switch on their lights, open doors, drive wheelchairs, even operate a telephone.'

'She'll use a wheelchair?'

'Yes, that ought to be possible.'

A terrible, constricting weight began loosening round me. 'She'll be able to go home?' Home was a place I had invented for her now: a converted cottage with ramps and these breath-operated appliances. It would take time to adjust and automate, but it would be done.

The doctor said: 'I'm afraid one of the problems with Cervical Two patients is that the respiratory muscles are paralysed. She's had to be given a tracheotomy. That means a tube inserted here' – he touched the notch under his throat – 'to connect her with an artificial respirator.'

'She'll always be on that?'

'Yes.' He removed his spectacles as if he no longer wanted to see. 'So you realise these cases require highly specialised nursing. The kidneys are in constant danger from infected urine. With a catheter in the bladder this can happen every four or five weeks. It can be fatal.'

The weight had closed round me again. In this numbness, it was the only measure of my commotion. 'Must she have a catheter?'

'With females it's very difficult. In these patients the bladder isn't contracting properly. Even with incontinence pads, soggy skin brings on pressure sores.'

She had become 'these patients' or 'females'. But if I were in his job, I thought, I would talk like a medical lexicon too. You couldn't function otherwise. Even for me, Clara had unfocused into a maze of life-support tubes. I could scarcely imagine what she was undergoing.

I asked: 'Does she know?'

'That's difficult to say. She hasn't asked. Patients rarely do. But I think she suspects.' He looked at me a little curiously. 'I'm struck by how composed she is. She seems a very brave young woman. She was a trapeze artist, wasn't she?'

'Yes, she was.' Unimaginable that this was past. Who was she now, without it?

'Some tetraplegics', he said, 'come to deny their own bodies. Perhaps the humiliation is too much for them. I don't know. They claim that because they can't feel the body, it's not theirs. But I don't think she's like that. I think she's one of those who'll want to understand their condition, and face it.'

'Yes.'

He made as if to stand up, but didn't. 'I should tell you, before you see her, that she's undergoing traction. This should realign her spinal column so that the vertebrae fuse. She'll be rid of it in six weeks, but it will look unfamiliar to you. She has to lie flat. Basically it means that weights have been attached to her head by a system of steel tongs drilled into the temples – '

'What?'

'It sounds crude, I know, but it's quite painless. You may also notice . . .'

Something gave way in me then. I don't think I was

understanding anything any more. Clara had dwindled to a head; and now even this was being drilled. I was suddenly weeping, but constrictedly, as if inside me. My head was down and the doctor did not see. I realised what he was saying, but could no longer organise it. I was lost in the labyrinth of her suffering. Even her body was not really passive at all, but seethed with potential infection. She would be spoon-fed always – there were no machines for that; she was suffering involuntary spasms of her legs; she would have to endure root pain from the damaged nerve-ends in her neck, always, there was no cure . . .

After a while I felt he was trying to lead me to a question, and since anything seemed better than this, I asked almost angrily: 'What is her future?'

The distance entered his voice. 'These patients suffer chest as well as kidney infection. They usually die within two to three years. Pneumonias are the worst. Ultimately one of these will kill her.'

I went back through the wards I had seen before. The youths in wheelchairs were still watching their televisions. Some of them were laughing together, and joking with the nurses. The man with the baby-walker hovered in his cubicle. His feet were moving, in their way.

In Clara's ward the women gossiped in corners: paraplegics in wheelchairs, mostly old. Only her bed had been half curtained off, as if she already belonged somewhere else. The nurse said: 'She's awake,' and left me.

She was lying quite still. Her eyes were open and staring at the ceiling. The traction tongs sat on either side of her head. They looked like earphones. The hair round them had been shaved away. I looked down at her. As my face entered her field of vision, her eyelids shuddered and she let out a kind of whispering cry. In her face I could see her arms lifting to hold me. She said: 'Mark,' as if experimenting with the name. I bent down and kissed her lips, filled with relief that this was still possible. Fleetingly I wondered if I was carrying some germ which might destroy the delicate balance of her body. But her mouth clung to mine. Before, it had always been my lips which had stayed longer. But now, when I leant back, I saw her eyes burning with unspilt tears. She said: 'Don't leave me.'

'No!' I rooted my hands to either side of her shoulders, and kept my face a foot above hers. 'What are you feeling like?'

'Just . . . light.' Then her eyes fixed mine with a bright, terrible fear, and she said: 'I'm paralysed, aren't I?'

I said: 'Not your face.' I caressed her cheeks. 'The rest, yes.' I covered her lips again with mine.

But after a moment she said: 'I knew I was,' and an odd calm came over her.

Her head stayed motionless in the traction, but her eyes followed me whenever I stirred. She said: 'Just now, I was sure my arms were coming up, and I'd see them holding you. But there was nothing.' Her mouth flickered. 'I feel they're still there.'

'They *are* there.'

'Yes, but you know.'

I took her hand almost from habit. But it was limp, cool. I was so used to it answering my touch, that it shocked me. I placed it gently back on the sheet. 'How long have you been conscious?'

She said: 'I don't know. I only half remember. They kept wheeling me under machines. I remember machines.' She frowned. The traction appeared to be pulling back the skin from her eyes, widening them. Her voice came wan but composed now, simply relieved that I was there. 'Lying here you just hear things. I could only see the ceiling. And now you.' She almost smiled. 'I don't know what happened.'

'Your forearm-brace broke.'

'I can only remember climbing the pole.' Her gaze strayed from me for the first time. 'Where have they gone now, the others?'

'The circus went on to Salisbury. They all left their love with you. They'll be coming as soon as they can.' I did not know when.

She said: 'The nurse told me I'd be out of this head-thing in six weeks.'

'Yes. The bones will be healed by then.' I noticed the tracheotomy tube entering between the buttons of her nightdress. I wondered if she knew it was there. The respirator was humming in a steel frame near my feet. 'After that you'll be able to sit up. You'll be looking around properly. What have you been eating?'

She said vaguely: 'I don't know. It tastes like cloth. They feed me all the time. In spoonfuls.' Her voice started to shake with self-disdain. 'They never leave you alone. This bed turns me all the time, all night. On and off my back, I think. I'm helpless. Twice yesterday a woman came. I saw her moving white things at the bottom of the bed – and it was my legs.'

She was close to tears. I kissed her eyes, her mouth. A fleck of blue make-up survived beneath one eyebrow, like a memory. I said: 'They're keeping the muscles stretched, and they have to exercise the joints.'

'But I'm helpless,' she said – and 'helpless' was the word which returned to her again and again, she whose body had been so poised, so controlled. The word was always to silence me, and slowly it made me afraid. She had invested so much in her self-sufficiency, in the looking-glass self she had once called her reality.

Standing above her now, I hated the coarse vitality of my own body, which I had never much noticed. I hated the way I stood over her (I had to) with my fists beside her shoulders, so commanding, so autonomous. Her own body lay under a sheet. I ached to run my hands over it, to knead it back into sensation almost brutally, by my own will, my love.

She said: 'I'm just . . . a *thing*, Mark.'

'You're still yourself . . .'

She did not hear. 'This morning a nurse came with wads of cellulose and started doing something under my sheet. I only realised what it was when the smell started. I think she ended by cleaning me out with her fingers.' Her face was flushed. 'They wash and comb me. Then they lift me up and examine me for sores. I don't want it, Mark.'

In a surge of panic I said: 'It'll get better. It's going to get better. You'll be in a wheelchair.' The words sounded grotesque even as I said them. 'You can look at television and listen to the radio. You can go on outings. You'll be able to read.' But all these comforts, as I spoke them, resolved into a passive desert of receiving. In them she could give out, do, create nothing. She looked up at me as if I hadn't spoken. I rushed on: 'You're the same person, Clara. Your essence hasn't changed. You've got your sight, your hearing.' I kissed her mouth to say: Even your sexuality isn't dead. 'When you're better I'll take you back.'

'Back where?'

'I'll find somewhere for us. They can do wonders for these places now.' In that moment I thought: yes, I'll take her back. But the next instant I knew she'd hate it. So that I would come to hate it too. I would live in terror of her body's fragility, of the knowledge that eventually it – and I – would fail her.

She said: 'You couldn't spend your time with me, not like this, not your life ...' She spoke it with such self-control, such practicality. Her returned strength astonished me. 'You'd stop loving me.'

I did not want her to see my face as I felt it becoming. I placed a chair beside her head and sat down. Her eye turned to watch me. The traction tongs sat in shaven circles on her temples, but a nurse had parted her hair in the centre and fluffed it over them.

Then there was a movement under her sheet. Something jerked forward. I thought I had imagined it. Then it happened again. She said: 'What are you looking at?'

'Is it your leg?'

'The nurse says it's spasms. I hate them.'

I stood up again and smiled down at her. 'Don't worry. There's nobody to see them.'

She said vehemently: 'I still hate it. Don't look at it.'

'I'm not.' I had rearranged my face into a facsimile of repose. 'I'm looking at you.'

But she said: 'Mark' – and the word held a tension of request which sank my heart. I knew what she was going to say. I think I had known from the first that she would say it. But I had not expected it so soon, nor spoken with such chill certainty. 'You will help me to go, won't you?' Her eyes glittered over me, hunting for my assent. '*Please.*'

Her calm mesmerised me. It seemed contagious. I said: 'Wait. Sometimes the feeling comes back. It sometimes does. After six weeks. So wait. You'll be more used to things by then.'

She said: 'I don't want to get used to things.'

'But wait. You will wait?' I covered her mouth with mine to stop it.

17

Never in my life, until the day she fell, had I restrained my emotions so harshly. But now they threatened to be fatal. If I could not coerce them, I would become intolerable to her. And I was all she had. So I concentrated on converting every energy into restraint, banter, optimism. It was perhaps the dawn of some maturity.

I rented a flat near the hospital. In time my job on the *Times* seemed to fall behind me so far – although it was only a few weeks – that I forgot it completely. I flouted the visiting hours and stayed with her through the day. She was regarded as a special case. Usually we simply talked, but sometimes I read to her, and occasionally we listened to the radio at her bedside, while my hand rested against her cheek. I forgot that her body existed. My love concentrated on her face; and there were times when I felt nothing but a grateful tranquillity, simply because she was there, herself. She was still very weak, but her voice gave out its familiar, musical calm, and sometimes she even joked, although her laughter, like her coughing, had grown bodiless, and tinkled in her mouth.

During six weeks she talked of the future only once, when she said: 'Provided I know I needn't go on, it's all right.' I took heart from this, thinking that the control of her future might reconcile her to the present. But I still remember how grimly her gaze lowered to her body as if she was determined, somehow, to be reunited with it. And each evening after I left, her bewilderment and loneliness came seeping back, and I would find them in her face next morning.

I would arrive after the ten o'clock inspection for pressure sores which so humiliated her, and when I fed her lunch in tiny spoonfuls – she was turned on her side – would try to convert the powdered eggs and feathery potatoes into a joke. Every half-hour I fed her sips of water – she was supposed to drink five pints a day, to flush through her body against infection – and at evening a nurse would assess her catheter bottle against a fluid balance sheet. Every three hours the electric bed turned her – from her right side, to her back, to her left side. Then I would move to anticipate her field of vision, and sometimes, when her face, cradled in steel and pillows, was tilted towards mine, I would get an answering erection, as if she were turning in bed quite naturally towards me.

By the third week the pallor in her face and voice had gone. But this resurgence of vitality brought a new distress. Beneath her self-control, when she spoke about the past – the circus or ourselves – a tense grief came beating up. Suddenly she would close her eyes and seem to drift away from me, dwindle to a profile talking at the ceiling, and I'd grow frightened. Then I would stare at her hand laid on the sheet before me, and will it to move. By my sheer resolve, it must move. Once I took it up and massaged it fiercely in mine, but its limpness became unbearable and at last I laid it back on the sheet. There it haunted me as a fragment of all her slackening body. I covered its spent fineness with a fold of the linen. And all the time she noticed nothing.

I could not augment her visitors either. Her nomad's life had left her few and scattered friends. An amiable couple arrived from the farm where the circus wintered, but they refused to understand her condition, and left saying they hoped she'd be on her feet again soon. Twice the Applebys and circus friends appeared, after motoring across three counties; but after an hour they had to return for the afternoon show, and her momentary brightness vanished. I felt only a muted fury that they would not cancel their

128

shows, and stay; but Clara never questioned that the circus was more important than she was.

On the sixth week, which I dreaded, her traction was eased off and her head suddenly freed. I bought her favourite shampoo and she had a gentle hairwash. She was transferred to a bed which would gradually lever up her body forty-five degrees and lower her legs, and for the first time she was able to see around her. When the consultant appeared, she asked him almost casually whether any chance remained of her body control returning. He looked at her with his half-withheld sympathy, judged her courage, and replied that there was none. This moment passed with no remark between us. But soon afterwards she was carried away by four nurses to her bath, while a fifth carried her respirator, and I suffered with her the vertigo of her floating head, and saw its look of hatred and alarm.

Next day her bed lifted her upright for half an hour, and two patients wheeled themselves in to visit her. But they were old and engrossed by their own disabilities, and instead of feeling companionship she looked at them – as they wheeled complainingly about – only with a dulled wonder. As for me, they filled me with resentment. In the atrocious lottery of spinal fracture, an inch or two up or down that stepladder of nerves, and a person was transformed. A single vertebra lower, and Clara might have lived to be seventy. Five vertebrae beneath that, and the control of arms and hands would remain to her, as it did to these self-pitying fortunates in their wheelchairs.

Once or twice I tried playing a game with her, pretending that we were a species newly emerged on earth. We had no past, and we had never moved. We were simply eyes, mouth, ears. But the sights and sounds which regaled us, I said, could excite us for decades (and we'd even learnt to read). It was only comparison with the past that depleted us. And we didn't have one.

But she only laughed at this extravagance, and said: 'But I *haven't* just emerged on earth.'

I bought her a colour television to replace the hospital's black-and-white set, and she pretended to enjoy this. But by now she was often blinded by head-pains, and she would simply close her eyes. I complained to the consultant that she must have been encouraged upright too early, or that the polyurethane collar supporting her head was constricting her, but neither of these was the cause. She was being convulsed by root pains from the broken nerve-ends in her neck, and there was no cure. Painkillers had no effect, and strong drugs endangered her. So time and again her face would break out in sweat, where her body could not. It was a pain-sweat of cold, and nothing stopped it. The first time it recurred, I said: 'Is it your headache?'

She answered through clenched teeth: 'I'm *only* a head. My whole body is a head.' Then she gave up trying to describe the pain.

The next day, as we watched the television, she said wanly: 'I don't see the point of me. What's the point of me?' She spoke as if the question were a practical one. 'I'm just a thing that watches.' And I could feel her eyes on me, saying: *You will, won't you?*

In the days that followed – and now it was twelve weeks since her fall – I felt her reduced to a battlefield, where only my presence and her pain contended. I was all there was for her. But in a sense she needed me less than before. She had recovered her habitual self-control, and she saw her condition with a chill clarity. It was not memories which made such desolation in her, nor the absence of a future; it was not even the humiliation or the physical suffering. It was her helplessness: the reduction of her strength, her self-sufficiency, to this defenceless, waiting thing. She wanted to re-establish her control.

One morning, watching me, she said: 'I'm only making you suffer. You look ghastly.' I knew she was thinking: if I go, he'll be released. I had become another reason for her to make an end.

130

'I'm all right. I'm all right so long as you're here.'

She said: 'You must get back to your work, Mark, start again. You can't stay here any more than I can. If we were happy, if I was going to live, it would be different.' Her voice hoarsened in pity. 'You thought I didn't know I'll die?'

'Yes.'

'I've known for ages. I heard one of the nurses telling a student nurse when they were turning me. They thought I was asleep. "These ones only last a year or two," she said. "Then the pneumonia takes them. So you mustn't get too upset when they go. And she's such a sweet girl." Guess what annoyed me most about that? Being called a *sweet* girl. Even you never called me sweet. I felt like one of Mrs Appleby's pekes.'

I remember looking at her with appalled adoration. She was even joking about it. But she sensed what I was feeling and said: 'I can laugh because I know we can end it. You have to get on with your life, Mark. It's been three months now. You'll lose your job in a minute.'

Then I was overswept by a curious, unbearable loneliness. She seemed to consider her death so much more coolly, less tragically, than I did; and now she was fitting it in with my career. With her old habit of perceiving herself from the outside, she refused to regard her passing as very important.

As she lay half upright in her bed, her gaze came burning over me with its appeal, which only intensified as her root pains started again. For a second she lifted her face away from me in her old gesture of exclusion, and said: 'I've thought of two other ways of dying, but they're both painful.'

I stared round the ward: I supposed she conceived suffocating, or biting out her respirator tube. Then she returned herself to me, flushed, pleading. I pressed my cheek against hers. She said: 'I don't want to die like that. I want to die quietly. *Please.*' Suddenly she was like an animal crying to be set free. The head-pangs started breaking up her words, her thoughts. 'It's waking up that's worst. Everything's gone . . . There's not enough of me left. If it was you, there might be enough.' The tears were streaming down her cheeks. '*Please.*' She started to let out screaming gasps. '*Please!*'

She shut her eyes tight against me, the ceiling, everything. Just a head, weeping.

This morning the chaplain visits my cell while Morgan is in the infirmary. He is kindly and seems far away. He talks of a moral and loving God. But I have just read that passage in *The Brothers Karamazov* in which the rebel Ivan confronts the priest Alyosha. He recounts to him some cases reported in the newspapers of Dostoevsky's day: atrocities committed against small children. If this God were as he said, Ivan asks, how could He raise a universe – even perfect and eternal – whose foundations included the tortured death of a single tiny child?

And neither the priest, nor the prison chaplain, can answer.

A journalist friend knew of a chemist in Dieppe who sold barbiturates over the counter. They were more easily bought in France, he said.

On the way to the Newhaven ferry in the early morning I made a detour to the circus, which was camped on Lindfield green. I wanted to gather messages from her friends, and to persuade them to visit her again: anything to change her mind, delay.

I found the Applebys polishing saddles in the ringside tent. Everything looked unchanged. The same Indian warbonnets hung bedraggled from their hooks, with the same Mickey Mouse mask and, at the end, the full-length mirror, whose reflection I avoided. One by one the troupe filtered in around us. They were like a family in shock, awkward, silent. I had the impression that my arrival was unwelcome. They did not really want to think about her any more. Her accident threatened them. They were used to her absence now, and they had to go on. (They would go on for ever, of course.)

Appleby looked the same, but I interpreted his habitual pathos as a tribute to Clara. He was guilty, worried about his reputation. The merger deal had been called off, and he had a police enquiry on his hands. But the broken forearm-brace had been welded by a respectable firm, he said, there had been no 'criminal negligence'. 'She must have put a lot of pressure on it.'

I said cruelly, angrily: 'That's what it's meant to resist.'

'Tell her we're keeping her wagon for her,' Mrs Appleby said. 'Barry's been driving it. Everything's just as it was.'

I was grateful for this, squirrelling away every morsel of news I could uncover. Mrs Appleby looked embittered. She had visibly hardened. I liked her more. 'The dogs could have replaced her second spot,' she said. 'The dogs should have done it.'

'They couldn't fill three spots, dear.' Appleby's head drooped back towards me. 'We're buying in a Spanish perch-act now. Just a replacement. It won't be like Clara.'

Her slot was left blank for the moment, I heard, and a little speech about her injury put the audience in a hush, and doubtless made them feel in contact with real life.

'And how is she?' asked Mrs Appleby. 'Is there a change?'

I said: 'She's very depressed.'

She asked sharply: 'I hope she's not thinking of doing anything silly?'

Appleby said: 'She'd never do that.'

But his wife's pin-eyes were on me. 'She was never one for sitting down.'

I turned to the others for messages, and they busied themselves with cliché. Only Barry warmed me. He looked hurt, older. He said almost nothing.

Later I wandered around the animal tents, scribbling down the messages, embellishing a little, inventing one from the elephants. The smell of sawdust with damp, trampled grass still sickens me. The sheer littleness of it all was bewildering: that she had been part only of this, and that even this was carrying on without her, almost as before.

I found Appleby's daughter mucking out the horses. She had always been jealous. 'How's Clara, then?' She launched the enquiry from behind the same small eyes as her mother's. I hated her bloom, her unthinking mobility. Eventually she said: 'Well, there but for the grace of God . . .' but she saw my expression and stopped.

On the night ferry back from Dieppe, under a sky bleak with stars, I almost threw the capsules into the sea. But I knew what wretchedness would greet this, and I tried instead to imagine them as she did: as a painless reunion with herself. But for hours I just stared at my knuckles clenched on the ship's railings, while my mind went numb.

For a few, liberating minutes I think I hated her. If I had been in her place, I thought, her presence would have nourished me for as long as I could stay. I could not voluntarily have abandoned her. But for her, I was not enough. I was losing the battle with her pain. In fact there had never been any true battle at all. From the first, she had decided. In this moment's bitterness I longed for time to love her less, for a few years simply to grow used to her, to experience the grossness and friction of nursing a tetraplegic, which might stain her eventual dying with a shadow of relief.

I was muttering like a madman at the stars.

Recently, with the days closing in, and knowing how soon my release is coming, I have noticed the brilliance of stars beyond the barred window. There is no middle distance.

134

The window's height, and the perimeter wall, destroy that. Just my cell, and eternity.

I used to conceive this night sky as a talisman that some divinity was at work. But yesterday, in my endless reading, I finished a book on Darwinism, which explains that the galaxies, like us, are the product of survival evolution. Planets travelling too fast or slow to orbit round a sun either crash or spin out into deep space. They become part of a gigantic wreckage which has been wandering and disintegrating for aeons, unseen. So the survivors endure only because they have by chance fallen in with the gravitational fields around them.

They are not the jewels of God, but the orphans of natural selection.

I arrived at the hospital with a stock of stories and circus messages to amuse her. But when I turned into her ward I was confronted by her drawn-back curtains and an empty bed. A nurse behind me said: 'She's gone to Intensive Care. She was getting kidney infection.'

For three days, while her condition deteriorated, I was racked by a conviction of failure. She was moving towards death in the way she most dreaded: in incoherence and helplessness, the way from which I had promised to deliver her. Sometimes a tired relief seeped through me, that the matter was being taken out of my hands. Then inexorably, almost at once, I would feel the grief of our missed farewell, the smallest things we had left unsaid.

But after five days she returned, weakened. The consultant confirmed not only kidney infection, but septicaemia. Her life expectancy had dwindled to a few months. She was wheeled back into the ward one evening, half asleep, and the curtains drawn round her again.

I was allowed to stay with her. Around her closed eyes, when I looked down, the features were pinched and sunken, and suddenly, with a choked sadness, I saw her as the old woman she would never become. In that moment it was as if, after all, she had seen out all her natural years. Then her eyes glittered open, and the young face reassembled round them. 'You're there.' Her lips were dry and hot under mine. 'I thought I'd never see you again. I was in there . . . and all I could think was: I never said goodbye to you properly.'

She was alert in her weakness, with a bird's vitality. She had even taxed the doctors about her future. 'So I suppose it would end soon anyway . . .' But after a few minutes, as if it had been preying on her, she said: 'I don't want . . . to be taken away from you like that.' She was speaking with her old, musical control, which seemed to be soothing things, laying them to rest. She said: 'You did get them, didn't you?'

'Yes.'

Then a grateful peace came over her. She said: 'I couldn't bear another waking up, another morning . . .'

I felt my eyes sweating. Hers moved over me like huge lights in her sunk face. I ached to ask her: where will you be going? As if she might know. But she would only have answered that she couldn't tell. She had never envisaged the future. She had always lived in the present. And soon she was asking me not to join her weaker self, to help her to be strong.

But my own strength had dropped away. I heard my voice (I'm ashamed of it now) say: 'Don't you love me?'

'Of course I do.' She was too weak to pity me. 'But you'd have to face it soon.'

I said: 'I can't do it.'

Then her voice broke in a faint, brittle sound which I still recognised as anger. 'Why do you want to keep me alive? Just so you can look at me? It's only because I'm helpless that I'm still alive. I don't want to go back in that place. I don't want to die alone. Or helpless like that.' Her fury burnt out into tears. 'Oh Mark, I'm sorry. I'm so sorry . . . Don't desert me now. You must understand.'

I said: 'I do.'

'Well, then?' Without her relief, her sudden peace, it would have been unendurable. I didn't want her last memory to be of my face as it was, so I went to a basin and dashed it over with a handkerchief. Then I sat quite calmly beside her. I even smiled. With every few capsules and sips of water, she said: 'Thank you, thank you,' afraid that I might stop. Then she was quiet in her pillows.

'I'll stay with you until you're sleeping.'

She said: 'It won't act before half an hour, will it? It's two hours before the nurse comes to turn me, but she's used to turning me in my sleep. They won't know.' She didn't realise that I would have to disconnect her respirator too, or it would gently keep her alive. After a while she said almost girlishly: 'Thank you. *Thank you.* It was good before this happened, it was wonderful.'

She asked me to rearrange her hands. For a while we exchanged our love, which was all of importance, and towards the end, as she became drowsy, she simply said: 'My arms are round you,' and I kissed her until she fell asleep.

And so I freed her into the dark.

18

Her Majesty's prisons are not a promising field for rehabilitation, nor my post of prison chaplain an easy one.

Yesterday, while his cell-mate was away sick, I visited Mark Swabey, the ex-journalist convicted of manslaughter. He said the term 'manslaughter' sounded so strange to him that it did not focus any reality at all, and he refers instead to euthanasia, which translates 'a good death'.

I cannot tell if prison has changed him, but he appears robuster than when he arrived last year. He seems a very defined character – forceful and rather nervous – yet suddenly he would stare at me in his disconcerting way and declare that he was in some sense split or uprooted. I answered that his dislocation is the common experience of men in prison, but he shook his head as if I had said something irrelevant.

I have always found him exacting, and this time, too, I received the impression that he was asking me for assurances which, once given, he would then proceed to refute. It occurred to me then that I was hearing not only his own voice but this Clara's as well. It is not uncommon for people to keep faith with the deceased by endorsing their values. I remember that after the death of my father, to whom I was much attached, I started adopting not only his standpoints, but even his habits and mannerisms.

A similar phenomenon may account for some of Swabey's intransigence. He once told me that this girl would not endure paradise among 'all those swaddled infants' – a curious reference, I thought – and it is certainly hard to credit her with any distinction. As far as I can judge, she was little more than a circus waif. Even her bravery on the trapeze suggests that of so many juveniles nowadays: the unconsidered rashness of youth, which thinks it will never die. These acrobatic feats are all very well, but the sceptic may reasonably enquire: to where was she ascending, and what for? As for Swabey, I think that at his age he needs to come to terms with life. It is immature, I told him, not to accept the world a little as we find it, but he only turned on me with his sudden intolerance and informed me that he faced it more honestly than I did. Then he proceeded to question the existence of divine love by quoting from Dostoevsky, whom I have not read.

But even in this world we need some basic answers, otherwise the questions become insupportable, and I wonder where he is to find these answers outside, in the future. He said he had plenty of friends, mostly journalists I imagine, and an invalid mother. He mentioned too, with evident nostalgia, a girlfriend from his recent past. He called her, self-mockingly, his lost homeland. Curiously enough, I believe I have seen one of her stained-glass windows, a beautiful piece, in the hospital chapel where I minister. He says she has created many, most recently of the fall of Lucifer – from a reference in Isaiah, I think, which I could not quote for him at the time.

From all he says, his Katherine sounds a very well-adjusted and civilised girl, and I even hinted that he might rekindle the relationship. However, his habitual obstinacy immediately resurfaced, and he spoke of her in the same tone of voice as he uses when refusing what he calls my 'false consolations'.

The moment I returned to my office, of course, I remembered the quotation on Lucifer, but could not recall where it had fitted into our conversation: *Thou hast said in thine heart, I will ascend into heaven, I will exalt my throne above the stars of God.*

19

When I was told the date and time of my release, I waited for the outside to come alive in me. But I envisage only somewhere thin-textured. It seems to have no blood. This skylit gulley of steel now encloses everything material. All my movements have contracted to the limits of a catwalk, a queue.

News of my discharge has subtly distanced me from the others. They look at me with alienation or envy, and talk less. Brown stares straight through me as if I had already gone, and Drinkwater only says: 'You're one of the lucky ones,' as if prison were a betting-shop. To Morgan, above all, I have become contaminated with the outside, with reality. He doesn't even enquire about my going. He looks sallow after his gastritis, and turns up his transistor louder than before. He talks as if he and I will be leaving together in some vague future. Only when my elbow jogs his pot of lanolin, he flies into a temper and says he hopes his next cell-mate will be less half-arsed.

I climb onto the chair and peer through our window. Only the clouds change, and their shadows on the perimeter wall, but I strain my ears for noises which will help me to envisage the outside – the siren of an ambulance, a motorbike's exhaust. Yesterday evening, which was very still, a man was whistling in the invisible strip of wasteland beyond the wall. He must have been half a mile away, but the sound reached me with eerie clarity, so that I wondered who he was and where he was going.

What is unbearable is that I sometimes feel nothing at all. It is as if the warm weight of me had evaporated, or was an illusion. Then I think that after all I will re-enter the outside world without effort, as a ghost reverts to nowhere, and the future goes blank.

So my leaving becomes more frightening and more urgent. I must have grown as institutionalised as Morgan. Too much in me wants to stay inside – something she would have despised. But that's what these places do to you. You are incarcerated in your own weaknesses. Your walls become thicker by the hour. You grow debilitated for anywhere else. You must get out or die.

But I have still not overcome the sense that she is out there somewhere, and the fact that this is not true raises a wall beyond the prison's, harder to pass beyond.

Clara. I find this, in a book on pilgrimage: *Among the oldest visions of man, none is more persistent than the hope of re-embarking one day on a half-remembered journey. In loneliness he travels back through symbols – an icon, a statue, another human being – seeking in them an avenue to God, a fragment of his lost divinity.*

I should have shown that to the priest.

Every third evening I attend 'free association' sessions open to prisoners shortly before their release, or to lifers on compassionate grounds. This offers table tennis and darts, and the chance to watch a television.

Some of the screws take the opportunity to strike up a rapport with the prisoners, but most just watch us for trouble, and tonight we have three of the louts. The atmosphere, in any case, is tense. Two long-termers on the fours smashed up their cell yesterday and were taken to the Segregation Unit, and floutings of the catch-all 'Good Order and Discipline' rule have escalated infectiously. So the screws have grown edgy, and there's talk of reducing privileges. Several of the prisoners are already complaining that their visits have been cut below the statutory minimum.

I sit in front of the television, hoping for a domestic

drama or comedy, something to make me reconnect. But the others want football and it's as meaningless as the prattle of Morgan's radio. Those figures might be playing on another planet.

Lorrimer is alone, flicking darts into a board. I go over to challenge him, but he greets me with a glower of conspiracy and says: 'Let's get the chess.'

We find a quiet corner, and he takes the white pieces. He plays with practised aggression – within five moves he is threatening my king – but his attention wanders. I have my back to the screws, but his eyes monitor them over my shoulder. He's charged up. He says: 'Narrowed that roller like you said. It's a beaut now.'

I think: This fellow half killed a man, and I'm condoning his escape. I haven't even reasoned it out. It's just instinct. Or perhaps I'm only helping him kill himself. God knows what he plans. I just murmur: 'Good.' As he advances his knight, his shirtsleeves recede from a wrist tatooed with crossed daggers and 'Lucy'. I say: 'You're going to be a doddle to identify, Lorrimer. You're a walking art gallery.'

'Where I'm going that won't matter.' His stare flickers past my head, then back. 'You know anything about New Zealand, Swabey?'

'Never been.'

'It's a fantastic country. I seen it on TV. Some parts nobody even been in until recently.'

For a second I wonder if this is just another prisoner's daydream, but Lorrimer isn't Morgan. He goes on: 'I know a bloke in London who knocks out Kiwi passports for a coupla hundred bucks apiece. Scotty's got relatives in the south island. Dunedin. It's all Scots down there. I reckon I can get me a job as a mechanic. That's my trade. If I go at it heavy for three or four years, I can set up on my own.'

'I thought Auckland was the going place.'

'Scotty says the south island's better. There's too much unemployment in Auckland, he says, it's full of Fijians, sweated labour. So I'm for the south.'

142

'Going straight?'

'Out there it's like you were never crooked. But you know the fucking Scots. It's not easy money.' He turns quiet as a screw strolls past, then says: 'I need to get me a lass too. The old man's yelling for exercise.' He rucks up his crotch. 'I've just about had this old country. Reckon it's loused up. I'm for the farthest I can go.'

Some new excitement is sharpening his usual frustration. As he launches his queen (he hates tactical retreats) I even imagine his hand quivers. This morning I noticed him staring through the glass of the wing office, and it occurs to me that he was eyeing the list of officers' duties. It hangs there flagrantly, so that you can see who is on 'external' at the courts, who is on 'nights', who is on the 'gate'. Lorrimer knows all the screws by name.

His hand is hidden inside his shirt now. His eyes still focus over my shoulder. He says: 'If I loan you a rum chess piece, don't flash it about.'

'Okay.'

His hand emerges and places the roller on a vacant square beside my king. It looks deeper-grooved now, narrower. I turn it over. The jagged perforation has been honed smooth. He says: 'I got the rawhide.'

I nudge it back to him, and he returns it to his shirt. His gaze never leaves the screws. His eyes look hot, as if they might give him away. Suddenly I think: he's planning to go tonight.

I say: 'Will Scotty be with you?'

'No, he's only two years left. He's going back to Aberdeen. Got a stash of stuff he never fenced off.' Lorrimer's head lowers to the chessboard. Even now he's losing, he never abates his attack.

I don't expect him to answer, but I say: 'Where the hell do you keep a cable in this place? How are you going to fix it?'

His neck has disappeared into his shoulders. He might be

in the throes of some saturnine fever. He says: 'You wouldn't grass on me, Swabey?'

'No.' I stare back steadily. 'In any case, what's the point? I'm released next week.'

'No, reckon you wouldn't.' His voice drops. 'The cable's already been fixed for me.'

'Who on earth by?'

'By the South-Eastern Electricity Board.' He swings his bishop across the board. 'You're asking so many fucking questions, you've lost your knight.'

I understand now. Somewhere there must be a power cable stretching from the roof to the out. If he can break through his cell ceiling in a night – and the mortar's probably soft in this place – he might make it. I try: 'You'll have to do it in one hit.'

'Yeah.'

Now I know he plans to go tonight. He trusts me, I think, but he wouldn't take a risk. The usual way to grass is to leave an anonymous note in the letter-box outside wing office, but by the time that box is opened in the morning, he'll either be caught, or gone. I catch his eye across the chessboard, and he winks at me. I try to picture the roof's height from the ground. His excitement animates a suppressed boyishness in him, and suddenly he looks his age: just a kid of twenty-four. Above the pastel anonymity of his prison shirt his eyes are shining, as if he were poised for some youthful dare. I see a ninety-foot sheer drop to concrete. I say: 'Christ, Lorrimer, you're not really thinking of that? How d'you know that cable will hold. It may break off its insulators either end.'

But he says: 'I got it sussed.'

We go on playing. I notice how unsteady my hands are, worse than his. I'm suddenly saying: 'Fucking hell, are you trying to commit suicide?'

'Keep your voice down.' He leans over his pieces, closer. He half whispers: 'You want me to snuff it in *here*? Think I'm a no-hoper? If I can't have it big, I don't want it at all.

It's shit or bust.' Perhaps he's afraid that I'll grass on him after all, on a humanitarian excuse, because he goes on: 'What the fuck did you think I wanted that roller for, huh? Think I can't shin along a cable without one of those?'

I grimace at him, then at the chessboard. We're approaching stalemate. We get up and join the others, shuffling to evening lock-up. He says: 'Say one for me.'

The lights go out at ten o'clock, so I just lie staring at the grey curve of the ceiling, in near-darkness. Outside, a three-quarter moon has appeared, and turns our window into a blanched tunnel, while the clanging of the screws along the catwalk dies to a faraway tingling. Morgan's wheezing calms into snores. His blanketed body lies hunched against the wall. Once our judas-hole blinks open. But by midnight the silence is total, and I still can't sleep.

Yesterday I signed my release papers before the governor, and already I am mentally withdrawing from this place. It appears stranger, a little mad; yet nothing familiar arrives to replace it. So I go on lying in the dark and imagine it – like a vast hive under the moonlight, three hundred cells where the larvae fester and dream.

I try to assess how long it will take Lorrimer to burrow through one of these ceilings, and wonder what implement he's using. I scratch at the mortar between the whitened stones by my head. It flakes a little. I peer at my watch but can't discern the time. The moonlight has shifted in the window. Then I climb down and place a chair under the bars. It's one-thirty.

Outside, when I press my face against the iron, the yard rises into view like an empty theatre-set. The perimeter wall crosses it in a jet-black band. The tarmac glimmers below, the sky above. The bars are so recessed that I cannot see our own block at all. The world has simply separated into three solid planes: tarmac, wall, sky, where a huge moon hangs. I squeeze my temples between iron and stone, trying to get a wider view, but the planes only extend.

Gingerly I climb off the chair and cross to our chipped mirror. Morgan has taped up its broken corners. But I detach a segment, and when I slant it out through the bars, there leaps into reflection the whole moonlit gallery of the yard. If I tilt the glass down a fraction, the tarmac rises vertiginously in it. If I slant it back, our tiered windows rush up to the sky. But half way between, Lorrimer's cable appears. It drops from the roof in a thin diagonal, and vanishes above the black slab of the perimeter wall. It looks impossibly fragile: less like a cable than a hairline fracture in the glass.

It's two o'clock and I return to my bunk. There's no calculating if he'll even reach the roof. I empty my mind and turn against the wall – I've become sensitive to every light-change from the window – and at last fall into sleep. Perhaps because I do so little here, I often sleep fitfully. The air in the cells is static and dead, and so silent that even sleeping becomes self-conscious in it. Sometimes I spend hours in a limbo of drowsing and half-thoughts. It's more exhausting than the day. But tonight I must have slept more deeply, because I am woken out of dreamlessness by a noise like pages riffling.

A pigeon has arrived in the window. Its profile bobs and jerks. It must have flown from the roof. I clamber onto the chair and thrust out the scrap of mirror. But nothing shows below the filament of cable. The roof above is a steep cross-section of tiles and wire. I scrutinise it, but see nothing. The moonlight picks out mottled pigeons sleeping there, like balls of waste paper. I prop the glass in the window's embrasure, and settle to watch.

After ten minutes a faint voice alerts me. I can't locate its source. But when it sounds again, I realise that it does not come from outside at all but from Morgan. He is whimpering in his sleep. Perhaps he's been weeping every night and I've never heard it. He cries in long, wavering

146

sobs, which dribble one into the next. It sounds, for some reason, like the grieving of a man very old – far older than Morgan – over someone who has been there a long time, but has now gone.

I pad over and shake him. 'Hey, old sod. What's the worry?'

He stirs awake and tries to sit up. The blurred oval of his face wavers before mine in the dark. 'Jesus . . .' Then his head is buried on my chest. I am reminded bizarrely of Katherine, and my hands come up automatically to hold him. His dust of grey hair shakes against my mouth. I feel his tears on my neck. 'I can't take very much more . . .' His back trembles against my hands.

I say: 'You're doing all right. You'll be out in under two years.' But I know this solves nothing.

He goes quiet against me. 'There just isn't . . .

I try to hold him upright. His soft, cold hands arrive on my arms. 'You can make it.'

'When I look back . . .'

'Don't look back,' I say. Perhaps I'm talking to myself.

He starts to whimper again as I detach him. His forearms withdraw to his chest like a foetus's. 'It's nights that's worst.'

'You were dreaming. You had a bad dream.'

'Always do.' He swivels his feet shakily over the bunk-side. His breath smells of hootch. His hand clasps mine like a child's. 'You'll come and see me when I'm out, won't you?'

'Yes, of course.' I imagine Monopoly in Cricklewood.

He is starting to find his bearings. In this faint light I see the fleshy chaos of his face, its bloodshot eyes, turning slowly to check his props: tobacco, radio, spectacles, lanolin . . . He is locating strength. After a while he says: 'You're a straight shooter, Mark. You know, I think your girl shouldn't have asked you to do that.' He fumbles for his radio, then puts it back. 'After all, she still had all her senses, didn't she? She could eat and watch TV.' He dabs

147

at his eyes with his pyjama sleeve. 'Good excuse for enjoying yourself. I reckon I wouldn't have done that. I'd have kept going.'

'Yes, I think you would.'

'Thanks,' he says.

Then something clacks against the embrasure, continues falling in silence. I cross to the window and peer at my watch. It's three-thirty. Into the mirror's fragment there swims a scene awash with moonlight. The shadow of the wall has retracted, widening the tarmac valley beneath, and the moon stands at its zenith. Along the wall's summit the razor-wire has silvered to a crown of thorns. Then I focus the mirror on the roof. Lorrimer is crouched there by the end of the cable, and at that moment something starts to glide along it with a soundless momentum. It looks like an improvised bundle, and the cable sags with it. I can even make out the sliver of rawhide from which it is suspended, and the glint of the roller above.

Morgan says: 'What's up?'

'It's Lorrimer. He's going on the lam.'

I understand now. He is testing the cable's strength with a load of debris. Three-quarters way over, twenty feet before it vanishes beyond the perimeter wall, the bundle slows in its dipping trajectory and stops. Nothing sounds anywhere.

Morgan has dragged the other chair beside mine, and levered himself onto it. He steadies his spectacles with both hands, stares into the glass. 'He can't make it, can he?' His voice bleats with a doubting half-hope. 'He couldn't ever make it?'

Now the bundle has jerked into life again, and is travelling backwards against the laws of gravity. Lorrimer is reeling it in. I glimpse a filament of rawhide taut under the cable. Then the load shudders and disappears under the eaves.

Morgan is breathing harshly. 'He'll never make it.' He clambers abruptly off his chair and slumps onto his bunk.

He has recovered now. 'Never.' He snaps his spectacles into their box.

My arm is aching from holding out the glass. For minutes nothing happens. At any moment I expect to hear the screws' cry of 'One away!' and alarms breaking out all over the compound. But no sound comes, and Lorrimer seems to have vanished. Then, as I direct the mirror more fully onto our wall, I see an eerie sight. Out of every third or fourth cell window thrusts a hand like mine, white and glinting with glass. Along three banked tiers – forty, sixty, eighty feet up – the extended arms and slips of mirror waver and gleam as if in bodiless farewell.

Then he launches out. His legs interlock above the cable without gripping it, while his hands clasp the loop under the roller. Weightlessly, it seems, in silence, he glides eighty feet above the chasm. He looks less human than animal – a giant sloth swinging into oblivion. For long seconds his momentum continues unabated. Then he enters the cable's levelling trajectory, and starts inexorably to slow. Twenty feet before it reaches the wall, he stops. For an instant he seems confounded, and stays dangling, lit by the atrocious moon. The drop is forty feet. He trembles in the mirror in my hand. I feel sick. I imagine the swivel of a spotlight opening up.

But the next moment, quite smoothly, he has hauled himself along the cable's ascent, glided over the perimeter wall, and disappeared into the dark.

We wait for five, ten minutes, as if something more must happen. But nothing does. The roller hangs abandoned in the cable's dip. The moon goes on shining. One by one the windows retract their white arms, and I drop exhausted to the floor. Morgan is watching me from his bunk. I say: 'He's gone.'

He turns to face the wall. 'He won't get anywhere.'

I crawl under my blankets, but for a long time lie sleepless, bathed in relief. Steeped in that light and silence, apparently effortless, his escape might have passed only in my fragmented mirror.

20

The day of my release is a cool October morning. In Reception two new arrivals occupy cubicles side by side: one dogged and elderly, the other young and frightened. For the moment the officers are too busy on the telephones to pay them attention. I wait in one of the cell changing-rooms, while an orderly brings my civilian clothes. He lifts them from a cardboard box and leaves them beside me in a neat, half-familiar pile.

I strip off my blue-and-white shirt, grey trousers and poorly fitting shoes. They are so impersonal – they will clothe someone else next week – that I feel no different as I stand naked above them crumpled on the floor: No. 63176.

Then I start to pick curiously at my own pile. It is less than a year since I wore them, yet they belong to someone deceased. Gingerly I try on some thermal underwear, a pair of blue trousers. They are the clothes of a man who was already half obliterated when he came in here – check shirt, light pullover, a herring-bone jacket. Yet as I put them on, I seem to be putting on that man's faded responsibilities and choices. I dress with a sharp bewilder-ment. The jacket, with its battery of pockets, completes this process. I am re-entering my own history.

I collect the case which holds my belongings. A warden checks it through behind a counter, then pushes over my subsistence money, and a travel warrant for Peterhurst. I am escorted to the main gate, where the Senior Officer says goodbye. A rumour is circulating that Lorrimer has been recaptured, and I ask if this is true.

He says: 'We haven't heard for sure yet. A fellow of that description's been arrested in London. Identity not established, though.'

I remember 'Lucy' and the maze of tattoos. I would have thought him instantly identifiable. Perhaps this is another man. I say: 'Goodbye, then.'

'Goodbye.'

I pass through the gate and find myself walking down a suburban street. The sounds are all soft, unmetallic. A hazy sun stipples the paving-slabs under my feet. They are fractured, and edged with moss. On either side, stucco houses sit behind low walls in gardens of green lawn and shrubs. They are not only numbered but individually named; 'Fairview', 'Holywell Cottage', 'Hillbro'. In front of them, violently coloured cars are parked. Colour is everywhere. And women of different ages, and children. Above them all, a wash of cirrus cloud covers the whole sky, and between the houses the distance is breathtaking, out over a council estate to shallow hills.

I flinch at it, and rest against someone's wall. The ache is perfectly familiar now, only more precisely focused. Once or twice, waking in my cell in the early morning, I believed I could cultivate hating her – for imposing this on me, then deserting – and evade sorrow that way. But the feeling fades, of course, with its ugly spasm of relief, and things return as now: the distance which cannot include her, the women who are not her.

For the moment this wonder at my freedom, and this mourning, comprise my identity. But more must come. I walk past a sluice-gate over a stream shining among hazels, and enter the profusion of a shopping street. People are everywhere, in bright clothes, walking to the market, queueing for buses. There are girls in jeans, good-looking and less so; boys on bicycles. Even the gutters trickle with precious rubbish: silver paper, beer cans, twigs.

Occasionally a half glimpse of some passer-by startles me

151

with the notion that he is Morgan, or Drinkwater or Lorrimer, I don't know why.

I stare into the greengrocer's shop and see a dazing sight: rank on rank of brilliant, compartmentalised colour.

Then I arrive outside a cafe. It has place-mats, table-cloths and fat pots of salt and pepper. I go in. On my table is a china ash tray, intricately stamped with chrysanthemums and little gold birds. The menu offers steak, cod and chips, lasagne, jacket potatoes, beef curry, apple pie, pancakes . . . In this palace I am the only customer.

'What would you like?'

I stare at her. Nobody has asked me that for a year. Her voice reminds me a little of Clara's. But the lasagne which I order tastes bland, like a prison lunch.

Outside, when I leave, the air is a miracle of movement, but no one seems to notice. It ruffles trees and people's hair. I wonder whether to catch a bus to the railway station, or to walk. It is the kind of everyday decision which I have unlearnt. The beat of my footfalls on the pavement implies a solidity I do not yet feel. So I take time off to admire a skeleton of red berries writhing up barbed wire. The sky is still covered with loosened scales of cloud – but I am growing used to this now – and beneath it the road descends to the station, between slate-coloured houses and a glimpse of wooded hills.